D1522096

Wrong Turn on Stockton Place

J. Lee Graham

Acknowledgements: Many thanks to Ken Hornbeck and AK for their advice and feedback.
Cover Photograph: AK

Book Cover Design: Arash Jahani

For the two Daves, with gratitude.

"Most of the evil in this world is done by
people with good intentions."
T.S. Elliot

Contents

Chapter 1 7

Chapter 2 15

Chapter 3 19

Chapter 4 25

Chapter 5 27

Chapter 6 39

Chapter 7 51

Chapter 8 55

Chapter 9 59

Chapter 10 63

Chapter 11 65

Chapter 12 69

Chapter 13 73

Chapter 14 79

Chapter 15 85

Chapter 16 87

Chapter 18 97

Chapter 19 105

Chapter 20.. 113

Chapter 21.. 131

Chapter 22 139

Chapter 23.. 145

Chapter 24.. 147

Chapter 25.. 165

Chapter 26.. 179

Chapter 27.. 185

Chapter 28 195

Chapter 29 205

Chapter 30.. 219

Chapter 31.. 223

Chapter 32 229

Chapter 33.. 237

Chapter 34.. 239

Chapter 35.. 247

Chapter 1

May 6. Friday

Gwen Parker opened the door of her '75 Chevy Nova and emitted an unexpected grunt as she stepped out. Forty-three but felt eighty. Jesus, she was sick of opening the gym in a pre-dawn five days a week ache and fumbling with numbers and money and bills. Cape May at this hour, the barely beginning rays, the faint nearly dark blue hitting the Victorians was like a pre-dawn Eden, but Gwen didn't see it much anymore. The cold early May that really wasn't cold compared to the wind off the water February or a damp, lumpish day in March, was invigorating and beautiful, but Gwen didn't feel that either.

For richer. For poorer. She and John started the men's gym twelve years ago, ("It's a sure hit, Gwen, there's nothing like it from here to Atlantic City!") And she believed him. It took a few years to have consistency. They worked like dogs increasing the membership, the place was open year-round adding expensive weekly rates for the summer visitors who actually paid it and were gone. Through flooding and insurance claims and revamping the office and painting the walls, to the day-to-day operation while keeping an eye out for drug dealing, the business grew. A solid reliable reputation was everything.

Now, she and John were minor celebrities in this odd Gemini-like town. In summer, it was almost unrecognizable with baby-oiled tourists and umbrellas, and beach music and the switch turned off on Labor Day, flipping back to a settled calm, a refocus to the haunted preserved historic homes, the ones that survived, and the unfeeling, ongoing demolitions for the ones that didn't. It seemed the craze for better hotels and miniature golf courses and swankier restaurants were making developers, in 1977, blind to what they were ruining. Gwen and others, in grassroots organizations and connections to higher ups were able to stop what looked to be the whole town from being bull-dozed under. Some rich hogs called creating never before streets and neighborhoods a much-needed renewal, others called Cape May, - "the island", - the loss of blue-collared innocence.

The gym held out. Male clients only, Gwen knew where the demolition ball lay and it wasn't going to hit here. The building on Stockton Place was in a surprisingly open area. No homes brushed up against it, no hotels, no ice cream stands, they were all on the water. This block was seedy enough to warrant people not to build near it. The gym's driveway only for one car, most members walked here or parked on the street. Simple, clean, one entrance, no front shop windows, a single solid door to a "man's place" as Gwen heard over and over "to get away from the missus, or the mistress, or the bitch girlfriend," and other names that made her cringe when she used to work the front counter during the height of the day.

Now, John does that. She comes in before dawn and holes up in the back office and does the books. At 6 AM, the official open for business time begins and she'll sit behind the register, checking membership, saying hello to the same group who are up with the dawn, coming in almost every day. John strolls in at 10:00, and she strolls out.

The dark entrance was almost pitch black and she felt around for the key hole with her fingers, practically blind until she got the placement right and put the key in the lock. The key slid in and unlocked the bolt. As Gwen pulled out the key and opened the solid door, something caught her eye. Rather, her ears. She stopped, door still open in her frozen hand, her ears listening, listening. Something wasn't copacetic. On the right was the reception desk, despite the darkness, she knew how many steps it took to land there, and behind that was the door to the office. She slid in, barely a sound, thinking if this were a robbery, she didn't want to tamper with any fingerprints. Hell, the door was a lost cause. She froze in the darkness of the gym, the morning light yet touching the tall windows. She opened her eyes wider trying to look at everything, as if she were coming here for the first time. Her eyes got used to the dark and the shapes of things began to take their routine placement.

The registration book was closed, pens neatly stacked. The door to the office was closed and she crept over, and listened at the door. Nothing. Something. Yes, something. She couldn't place it, but some sound was there, in the gym, in the walls, in the office? Rats? Something in the walls? 'Good god, it's an office!' She got mad at her own fear and bracing for an attack turned the handle and pushed the door open ready to scream or fight.

Darkness with a tinge of vague blue on the one window, tiny, fit for a small dog. She flipped on the single light switch she had flipped a million times.

Nothing.

The desk was as it always was. Papers and accounting books and ledgers, all in a pile. The file cabinet was closed and she saw the lock hadn't been tampered with. The safe was there solid. Stillness.

But then… there it was, this sound, this odd, continuous sound that didn't belong. Gwen picked up the phone to call John, but hung up. What was she going to say? There's a sound. There's this sound, John, and it doesn't stop and yet, I can't tell where it is.

"Go find it,' would be his exasperated reply.

Gwen returned to the reception desk which was the beginning of the gym's single large room. There were three light switches on the wall and she picked the middle one and turned it on expecting gunfire.

The weights and machines were in their place and Wendell had done his usual clean job last night of stacking everything back and wiping off the benches and the mirrors. The two trashcans were, it seemed to Gwen, emptied, from what she could tell, and placed in the two typical corners. Beyond the gym was a small hallway that led to the locker room in the back. She cocked her head as she walked toward it. There was a sound, and it was in the locker room. Christ, she hadn't been in that cold smelly locker room since she and John repainted it two years ago. If a pipe had broken or if the benches were shabby, John or Wendell would know and the only thing they'd ask her was if there was enough money to fix the damn thing.

She edged slowly. The gym had six windows, placed high in the wall, but none were open and none were broken. The only other door to the gym was in the far back corner and even though it was a fire hazard, she and John always kept it locked. She tried it anyway. It was still locked.

That sound! She moved into the empty hallway. There was no door to the locker room, only an archway and she stood there and listened. Christ! It was the sound of a shower. Somebody was taking a shower! There were two frosted windows in here, placed mid-way up the wall and the feeble light created a darker tone, murky, like swimming at the bottom of a lake.

Gwen veered back into her mind to replay her morning. The front door had been locked. She knew because she had

11

to press a little harder than natural to make the bolt unlock when she turned it. The windows were all intact, no broken glass or oddly felt current of air. Wendell had locked up last night after he cleaned. Yet someone was taking a shower.

Gwen's creaky tired attitude about men's gyms and men's money and men's sweat and privilege that had always irritated her yet gave her a comfortable life vanished. A tinge of excitement zinged through her and her private fantasy about the Coast Guard joggers seen on Pittsburgh every day now naked, showering, unsuspecting.

She mentally slapped herself and walked silently passed the last of the locker rows to the shower area. There were two showers each in their own stall. Each had a curtain to use for privacy and often the men didn't bother to close it due to all the water it splayed on the floor. John complained about it, but Gwen shrugged. Men were pigs.

On her left, toward the toilets, one lonely bench had a pile of clothes. Gwen saw the sneakers, socks, the pants, shirt, gym shorts stacked up like a teenaged kid's dirty laundry.

The running shower stall's curtain was closed. The gym owner took a step, and another. "Hello!" she called, making her voice louder than the pounding waterfall. "Hello! Who are you? How did you get in here?"

Silence. Water falling, splashing repeatedly off the wall and the floor.

"*Hello!*" she repeated, now getting irritated at being ignored. "What are you doing here?"

Nothing. That infernal shower, that wasted water pouring and pouring probably for nine hours and Gwen saw an exorbitant water bill in June. Christ, I bet Wendell was using this to clean the floor and forgot to turn it off. God, how could he forget to turn the damn thing *off*?

Gwen marched over and yanked back the curtain. She reached for the knobs and jumped back like a cobra had struck her. The naked body of a young man was crumpled on the floor, his head bashed in, a weight next to where his brain should have been. The water from the shower splashed on the body and bounced off and with the curtain being freed, the water now splashed on Gwen. She screamed for what felt like eternity and the last thing she saw as she ran out of the room was the blood trickling down the man's face into his mouth or swirling down the drain.

Chapter 2

*T*he *bookstores are dying, Kip. People read on small screens they carry in their purse; they read on their phones, in a box the size of a coaster. Remember coasters? I knew it the moment the skinny 23-year-old kid with the shaggy beard mumbled something when I asked him for a copy of* THE QUIET AMERICAN. *He knew the book, which surprised me, but he rolled his eyes when I asked him to speak up and enunciate since this old doddering person standing before him clearly wasn't worth the effort or the time. He was the new type of boy now, Kip, skinny rebel but with a half -grown beard, some sub-category of man, I suppose. They must have a name, that generation, but I gave up keeping up long ago. The thin worker didn't repeat himself, just sighed, raced around the counter to a tiny section called Vietnam classics which I guess, from his point of view, deserved its own shelf, leaned over in an irritated, 'here, I'll get it for you' way, and thrusted it in my hands.*

"How come this isn't in the general classics section?" I asked, but again, his mumbled tone was lost on me, another eye roll, and off he twisted to the register again, only to sit on a stool and looked out the window, bored, waiting for lunch, wishing he could smoke a cigarette.

There's no bookstore on the island anymore, Kip. I have to drive to LBI for this last holdout; there's nothing beyond this for almost fifty miles. Books are online now, readable, orderable, and I applaud the convenience, but I miss the atmosphere. I miss the getting lost in the shelves. I miss you.

The rebel beard was the stark reminder. Remember how we used to say the ocean would be crashing on this shore for eons after we're gone, and we'd laugh at the impossibility of that reality, how we'd be 'gone', as if the earth could keep on spinning, or surviving without us. You were gone way too soon, but it was the obnoxious book shop boy who made me open my page and write. The stories are there and must be preserved. Cape May in the '70s. The way it was. The way we were. I know that if I don't write them down: these fantastic murders and these fantastic adventures, no one would believe the intimate details. They can find the bare bones, so to speak, on any website, the names of the victims and the person who killed them, but not the mores, not the times. Those are erased. Nowadays, no one does research for the flavor of the era, now it's only a soundbite or a quick Wikipedia look, a three-sentence summary.

You and I and this town, and this beach and this place are not a three-sentence summary. The victims are not a sound bite, an anecdote to be relayed during happy hour in some beachfront shack where loud music overshadows any sense of camaraderie or connection.

The beaches have changed; Cape May has changed. It's gotten smaller. The Jersey shore has gotten smaller. The hurricanes are destroying it little by little and no matter how much sand they ship in, one of these days a storm will be large enough to wipe us all off the map. The large monstrosities called second homes dominate the shoreline and I can't help but secretly chuckle when after this last storm, the one that made the headlines, pictures flashed all over the internet of the McMansions crushed, missing their first two stories, pitched forward. Often the front pillars that supported them were missing, making the houses tilt toward the rising sun as if on bended knee, asking forgiveness for taking up so much space and destroying so much of the environment. Four car garages now, Kip, in some of them. You can't imagine the effrontery, the sense of entitlement that often accompanies these people, these homes. The beach where we spread your ashes is gone. It was too remote for anyone to care about replenishing, it belonged to the ocean and there was no use fighting it. As did you.

But remember in 1977, it was the place I most loved to swim, to hang out, and later, I introduced it to you and you said it was heaven on earth, the dark end of a long tail of a beach, no homes in sight.

Chapter 3

G wen Parker, after seeing the body, ran to the front desk and called the police. Her stammered shivering words were incoherent at times. "Help… shower… Alex, locker room, blood, help, hurry" A moment of listening, then "Cape May Gym" Hung up.

When the patrolman knocked on the solid opaque door, she knew by the timid sound it was Sargent Ricca, the local cop. "It's open," she was barely breathing. He appeared, always the gentleman, his hat off, tipping his head in a cautious hello. Gwen was behind the desk glassy eyed.

"Mrs. Parker, you called the police?" The young cop sized up the place, saw nothing strange. "Are you in danger?" He had his hands ready for either Gwen Parker drawing a gun or fainting.

Gwen's idea of a cop was never going to be Peter Ricca, he looked as scared as she was. He was trying to appear confident and strong, but he hadn't much experience with frightened phone calls at dawn. He mostly handed out parking tickets or did security at the high school prom.

"Pete, thanks for coming so fast," Gwen said. "He's in the locker room," she nodded toward the back of the gym.

"Who is?" Pete asked. "You're not open yet."

Gwen mentally stared at his imbecility, thinking *didn't you get my message?* She cut him some slack knowing he was bouncing off of nerves.

"Alex's in the back, taking a shower," she said, wanting to jump into a joke because that was her natural response to shock. "He's dead, somebody killed him."

The cop went back, saw the blood, checked the man for a pulse, called the ambulance, called in MacNeil the only detective in this small town, and sat with Gwen until MacNeil arrived. Nothing took long. The looky-loos, the press, the tv cameras, the gossip, hard to ignore or stifle in a town this size were out in droves by 6 AM.

Sgt. Ricca's guarded presence as he stood at the entrance to the gym elevated the neighbors' curiosity vibrations to a new frequency. To Detective MacNeil, it had the hum of a game show audience, the chatter, the excitement, people hoping their name would be called.

"Maybe they'll ask me questions," he heard one woman say rather loudly, "I live right across the street."

"Did you hear anything?" the woman next to her asked with a look that said, *I hope so*!

"Well, maybe I did and maybe I didn't, but that's for the cops to ask me. I'll be here irregardless. They know where to find me."

MacNeil winced. *No such word as irregardless, babe.* He followed Ricca to the locker room.

Detective Christopher MacNeil wasn't used to staged murders. His eight years of this work showed him a myriad of robberies, once in a while an ugly mugging in an alley, vandalism, break-ins, stolen cars, and the occasional sad tawdry impulsive murder done in a fit of rage and too much booze.

This was something almost theatrical. The man looked in his mid-20's, hard to see his face with half of it crushed in, but overall he looked strong, healthy, lying in a helpless, guarded position, his left hand around his head, his right flung out, open, the water still splashing on his chest and stomach.

"Alex," he said. "Alex who?"

"Kearney," Pete Ricca told him. "Trainer here, John and Gwen hired him to bring in more business. He's been here since last September."

"How do you know this?" MacNeil didn't even turn his head, kept looking at Alex, studying the position of the body, the 35-pound free weight lying near his left leg.

"It's Cape May, sir. I grew up here. Only men's gym in town."

21

Chris MacNeil had been in Cape May for two weeks. Late April to find a place, get his bearings, buy groceries, set up utilities. May 2nd, first day on the job, his too cheerful boss showing him around introduced as the new hire, the new guy in town, the staff looks, the other policemen sizing him up, practically sniffing him looking for a weak spot. He wanted a small town where he'd be the only detective on the payroll and getting walloped with a murder - which although completely plausible - was not what he was expecting on his third day at work. He barely knew where the typing paper was to make out a report.

Detective MacNeil told Ricca to open up the lockers and look for anything that might be important. MacNeil examined the heap of clothes on the bench nearest the shower area. Left where Gwen saw them were a pair of jeans, t-shirt, socks, sneakers, gym shorts and underwear. Wearing plastic gloves, he pulled out the jeans and held them up.

"I think these are Alex's clothes," he said to the coroner. "You think they match his body?"

The coroner was kneeling over Alex, looked at the length of the jean leg, back to Alex. "Could be, Detective." The man continued his report, confirming officially he was dead, had been for about eight hours, killed sometime between 10 PM and midnight.

MacNeil searched the pockets and found a set of car keys: one for the ignition and one for the trunk, a third key that could be for anything. In the back pocket was Alex's wallet. It held $6 dollars in cash and a New Jersey license with Alex Kearney's signature on it. No photographs, no cards, nothing. The license read that he lived on Oregon Street in the Villas.

"You know Oregon Street?" he asked the coroner. "What kind of neighborhood is that?"

"Blue-collar, small, mostly families," the man grunted trying to be respectful to this new guy he'd be working with but hated the interruption.

"Sgt," MacNeil said handing Ricca the keys, "find Alex Kearney's car. It's probably parked outside. Ask Gwen if she knows what his car looks like."

The crime photographer moved around them like a dancer, taking shots of the room from all different angles, and the coroner backed off so he could shoot Alex and the free weight.

"So the cause of death was that weight smashing his skull? Detective MacNeil asked. "Sorry doc for the lack of delicacy, but that's the bottom line, right?"

"Yeah, from the look of it, the autopsy'll tell me more, but Detective, hang on, there's also this." He motioned the photographer to make sure he had shot the body. He squatted next to the corpse and opened Alex's legs. A large pool of blood oozed out of his groin.

"Jesus," MacNeil whistled under his breath, "somebody crushed his nuts."

Chapter 4

You should see the crime scene now, Kip. A new age spa for the richer tourists. Locals don't go there too often as far as I know, but hell, nobody talks to me anyway. Library volunteer with too much time on his hands. Part-time to boot. I'm rolling over into an hourly wage starting next month. Wow, moving on up. Not bitter, Kip, I can hear you now. Just reality.

You liked to play the 'remember when' game when you were feeling down. "Remember when I met you for the first time?"

I do, Kip. I was busy counting money and you walked in. I looked up and said to myself, "Oh, there you are."

The certainty. The absolute eternity of it.

"That's it?" Your stupid tilted smile.

You wanted me to gush and I couldn't help but respond. Your brown eyes and straight hair. The 6'2" of you. The baby face that made so many people say, "You're 32? You don't look older than 21!" The slim body with your hairy arms and legs and chest that deserved to be wrestled to the ground whenever you read a magazine or opened a letter and threw me that egotistical glance.

Kip, this world has changed incredibly. It's easier now for the younger guys, some of them anyway. They come out. There are TV shows and more and more movies and last winter even Hallmark put out a holiday film full of ungodly unrealistic, plastic stereotypes, but hey, the leads were gay. So, to hell with unhealthy holiday expectations, the gays are being represented. A hard construct to wrap my head around.

You would have said, "I couldn't be bothered."

Chapter 5

MacNeil's bat-like hearing and his attention to detail were two of the many qualities that landed him this job. He had a solid presence, most of it a pretense, but studied well, used to illicit information. His bedroom eyes exuded charm, his eyebrows were suave and dark. He cultivated a sexy swagger when needed, a trusting face at other times, but overall, he had a commanding voice that became a penetrating laser beam when irritated. Eight years working in Buck's County mostly got him tangled with robberies and vandalism, but more necessary was the finesse he used with haughty actors, rich, entitled landowners, political allies of said landowners and the continued stress of citizens' wanting their most recent little mess cleaned up, rather, immediately.

"Comes with the job, Chris," his supervisor used to say. "you're a single guy. You can't handle it alone. Get married, you need a wife who'll listen to you."

"Thanks," Detective MacNeil countered. "As if that's her function, her only reason to be with me, to be the dumping pot of a long day."

"Well, it's better than nothing, than drinking yourself to death, to shooting yourself in the head, to-"

MacNeil usually gave a small salute with his hand and walked out the door.

Now, he sat opposite Gwen Parker in the tiny office, door closed. The window was open for a crack because Gwen wanted to smoke.

"Mrs. Parker, my name is MacNeil, Detective MacNeil. Can I ask you a few questions?"

Gwen looked him over, surprised at how handsome he was. He had heard him plunder into the gym, but she hadn't greeted him. Peter Ricca asked her to stay in the office until they were ready to question her. "Don't want you touching anything," he said almost apologetically.

"Alex's car is parked on the street, it's a red '71 Chevy Vega," Ricca said handing back the keys.

"Did you look inside?"

The Sargent hesitated, "No, I thought you would want to do that. There are too many people out there snooping around, I had to push them back, get their footprints off the grass. If I had opened that car, they'd be flocking up on the hood."

"Thanks, Ricca, I'll do it later. Take notes for me, will ya?"

"Mrs. Parker," MacNeil started, "you got here at what time?"

"5:20. The gym opens at 6:00, and I always arrive early to go over the paperwork, get the drawer ready for the day, set up a deposit, check yesterday's mail." She looked at MacNeil with a 'you want me to go on with this bullshit?' daring him to challenge her. "I put on a fresh pot of coffee and drink in the silence. I hate it."

"Monday through Friday?"

"Yep. John comes in at ten and he opens on the weekends."

"When you came in this morning, was the front door locked"

"Like I told the cop, jeez don't you people talk to each other?"

"No, we don't."

Gwen sighed a bit dramatically, probably for his benefit as if to say, I'm too sophisticated for your childish games. She recited, "The door was locked. I took out the key and opened it and-"

"Did you see anything before you got to the door? Someone leaving? Someone sneaking around."

"If I had seen someone sneaking around, don't you think I would have said something?" It was her turn to be smart.

You ain't going to win, sweetie. Don't you even realize you're the top suspect?

"So, I unlock the door, like I do almost every day, and walk in. Lights out. Everything hunky dory. Except for that sound."

"What sound?"

"At first I didn't know what it was. It wasn't loud, back in the distance. I came in here," she gestured to the office, "and took off my jacket and put my purse on the desk, and listened because that sound never went away."

"Do you keep the office door locked?"

"No," she said still obsessed by the sound. "It's never locked. The safe over there is locked, but jeez if anyone wanted to get in here, it's an easy shove. The door is plywood and a couple of elbows would make a big enough hole."

"The sound."

"Yeah, well, it turned out to be the shower water running, but it frightened me because it didn't belong. Or I guess I never heard it before in a silent room. When you're in here all day, they're slamming the weights, even though John goes around and tells them not to, or they're grunting like hogs or clanging weights onto the bars. I've never heard the water before."

"So, you hear the water," MacNeil prompted.

"Like I told the officer, I follow it to the locker room, see the curtain closed, pull it open, really mad because I thought Wendell had checked everything, turned off a running shower for Christ's sake before he left, and there was Alex," she looked out the door. "Alex. Naked, gray, dead."

"How did you know he was dead?"

"You could tell. It was obvious. His body was gray. I never saw a dead person before, but I knew he was. He didn't moan or move, his eyes stared out at the wall." Gwen Parker wanted desperately to erase that image. "Alex, Jesus."

"How long have you known Alex?"

Gwen bristled. "Whaddya mean 'known'?" Gwen sometimes picked a battle when there was no war.

"How long has he been working here? What was he like? Did you know him before you hired him, what kind of man was he?" *Christ, lady, you're exhausting me with your counterattacks.*

Gwen kept her guard up, watching the man's brown eyes. They were focused. Didn't let up. She stared right back. She was used to the men not paying their membership and bullying her with excuses and then coming back with their instant misogynistic bullshit defense mechanisms called Round Two. She didn't budge an inch, not with them, not with this guy.

"Alex is the, was, the trainer here. We hired him, John and I, last September. There was an increase in membership, some of them (the ones not too macho and stuck up) asking for advice about lifting, losing weight, gaining muscle, that sort of thing. John couldn't hold all their hands, so we hired Alex. He was a nice guy. He worked here on Saturdays and Sundays, but the rest of the time it was as needed. Meaning, if a guy set up an appointment with Alex, they figured out the times between themselves. The man paid us for the training and 75% of that went to Alex."

"Did his clients ever complain about him?"

"Complain?"

"Disgruntled, 'he's a waste of money,' 'didn't teach me anything'."

31

"No, not that I heard. John might have heard something; most people here don't talk to me about things like that."

"Do you have a picture of Alex?"

"No, why should I?"

"For a brochure on the place, advertising, a newspaper column introducing him to the gym." His voice turned. "God, why are you so defensive!?"

"I don't like what you're insinuating, Detective," Gwen snapped.

"Do you want me to wait until your husband arrives?"

"I'm perfectly capable of handling my own questions," she said. "When you work in a place like this, the men can climb all over you if you let them. The one-liners, the innuendos, the eyes looking at me. The stupidity of it all gets to you after a while."

"So why don't you quit? You don't sound very happy."

"Quit? No, I'm not quitting. This is Cape May, Detective, this is my home. I'm on committees to see this town doesn't get plowed under for a roller coaster, and in the long run, this business is my tie to the town. People know me. The gym is a good draw; it's doing well. I wear a different hat when I'm in here, Detective, and some of the men actually are gentlemen."

"Do you know of anyone who might kill Alex?"

"No."

"Did you ever see him get into an argument with a client while they were training?"

"No, but John might have."

"Did you like Alex?"

Gwen paused. "Nobody's perfect, Detective. Yeah, I liked him. I didn't see him too often, I don't work on the weekends, but he knew his training. He was strong, he could take care of himself," she stopped. "Well, clearly not. Everybody has a weak spot, right Detective?"

"Yes, they do."

"I may not know people personally, but I can intuit them. I know how they feel when they walk in here, whether their day was good or bad or if they feel lonely or depressed or happy or a myriad of other emotions. I don't ask them questions, Detective, I'm not their analyst. But I feel it. With Alex, he sometimes didn't walk in here, he strutted. There was a hidden cockiness, that he carried. I mean, why not, he's a, was, a good-looking guy. He was strong and once in a while he would show off and do incredible, almost acrobatic stunts on the bars, but then he'd switch gears, seem almost embarrassed, turned red, and became extremely humble about it."

Gwen drifted for a second as if remembering something. "But other times, he strutted in here like he owned a harem or won a million bucks up at the casinos. It wasn't anything he said, but the way he regarded me or John, it was cold and dismissive. Once in a while he would pass by and look right through me," she paused, shaking her head, "and Jesus, that made me want to reach over the counter and knock his brains out."

MacNeil said nothing. He waited another fifteen seconds to see if she had anything more to say. Something had gotten under her skin; some memory had her upset. He'd find out. Eventually. Not today, perhaps, but eventually.

"You mentioned a 'Wendell'," he prodded.

Gwen switched faces. "Wendell Taylor is the janitor here. He closes up each night and then cleans the place. Wipes the benches, uses bleach for the locker room, checks for fungus and crap in the showers and the crap in the toilets. Men are pigs," she caught herself, "well, maybe not all men, but in a bathroom, they are pigs. Wendell was used to it, it didn't bother him, but man, the smell, the toilets, men don't aim, Detective, not when they don't have to. And the lockers themselves reeked of sweat and t-shirts and underwear and Christ, how do you live with each other?"

Gwen stopped herself and her tirade and Detective MacNeil wondered at whom she was really talking about.

"How long has Wendell been working here?"

"Not too long, I'd say about two years. He helped John fix some plumbing and water leakage and John was smart enough to see someone of value."

"So he hired him to clean up a locker room?"

"Yeah, well, an overall handyman. Wendell's a lone wolf, always likes to work with no one bugging him, peering over his shoulder."

"What time did Wendell usually leave the gym?"

"I don't know."

"But he always locked it up when he left, is that correct?"

"Yes, as far as I know. He had a key."

"Who else has a key to the gym?"

"Wendell, of course, I do, John does and Alex. That's it."

MacNeil held up the mystery key from Alex's key chain. "Does this key fit the door?"

"No, that's not a gym key."

"How do you know?"

Silence. He counted to ten.

He was about to ask it again when she said, "Because I know what the fucking gym keys look like!"

"So, do you think Wendell forgot to lock the door last night?"

"I don't really know, Detective, you'd have to ask him."

John Parker entered the office, burst in it was more like it. He saw Gwen sitting behind the desk and a new cop, not in uniform, staring at her like it was a chess match. "Gwen, Jesus, are you alright?"

"I'm fine. I'm shaken up a bit, but nothing happened to me. Someone killed Alex."

"I know. You told me on the phone. How?"

The other man stood up. John met his eye. John was a strong looking man, wide shoulders, handsome build. MacNeil was taller than John by about three inches. He held out his hand. "Mr. Parker, I'm Detective Christopher MacNeil. I'm in charge of this case."

"You're new around here, right?"

"Yes, sir, started two weeks ago." Saying 'three days ago' sounded weak and apologetic.

Chris took note of the calloused hands. He imagined Mr. Parker could easily slam a weight on even a trainer like Alex Kearney. "Alex was hit in the head with a 35-pound weight." He purposely didn't mention the crushed balls.

"Jesus." He sat on the desk. "Alex," his breath continued like he wanted to add something but stopped himself. "Gwen had nothing to do with this, God, who the hell dumped Alex in here?"

"He wasn't dumped, John," Gwen interrupted, "he was already in here."

"How would you know that?" MacNeil looked at Gwen her face growing red.

"Well, I guess I don't, but who would carry someone like Alex into a building and then go through all that trouble to drag him into the shower, take off his clothes, and-" she remembered the brains on the shower stall floor.

"People will do a lot of things to get away with murder, Mrs. Parker," MacNeil said. "The killer might have had help."

"Help?"

"A two-person team, a husband-and-wife team, a couple of hoods, you never know."

"My wife was home with me last night," growled John Parker.

"Yeah, absolutely, the alibis of spouses are always fucking watertight, Mr. Parker."

MacNeil had reached his limit. He could sense the irritation in his voice getting out of hand. He wanted them separated. "Mr. Parker, let's go for a walk. I want to see the gym through your eyes, see if there is anything out of place."

John Parker was smart enough to keep his mouth shut and the sad look on his face when he looked at Gwen was one of resignation, surrender. This could ruin his business, and Christ, if there was anything he could do to turn back the clock and keep Alex from getting killed in his place, he would have done it.

Chapter 6

Detective MacNeil moved once again through the gym, double-checking for anything that could give him an answer. There were six windows, three on each side, that started four feet off the floor. They were large windows with small panes that rose a good six feet to the ceiling. On warm days, Gwen walked around with a long pole to lock into the loop of the window and pull the top half down a couple of feet. One day, three men lay on the benches pretending to lift weights so they could look up her skirt and when one of the men's balls popped out of his shorts, "accidentally", Gwen saw red. She pointed the pole at his nuts and said, "If that happens again, mister, I'll knock both of them in the corner pocket and you'll be kicked out of here for good."

After that, John opened and closed the windows.

"Were any of these windows left open?" MacNeil asked John who walked next to him.

"Unless Gwen closed it this morning, which I doubt," John Parker explained. "They wouldn't have been open in the first place, it's too cool outside."

Chris MacNeil judged the height, measured the distance to the floor and decided that an entry from up there would give a person a broken ankle or leg if he jumped. Unless he had help. "Is there a ladder around here?"

"In the locker room," John nodded his head in that direction. "An eight-footer."

"You got a clean place here, Mr. Parker. I want to check with the Health Department to see if there were any complaints filed, but I'm impressed. I've been to gyms in New York and Philly and a lot of them are pretty rank." He bent down along the wall under the windows looking for any scrape or leather markings of a ladder or shoes. There was nothing.

"Thank you, Detective, I guess," John shrugged. All he saw was a drop in membership as people didn't want to be connected to a murder scene.

MacNeil noticed a certain organization to the weights. Each bench had the same particular grouping of weights: the heavier ones on the bottom and then stacked to get progressively lighter. "Where did the 35-pound weight go?" he asked.

John did a very quick scan and pointed to the second bench from the back hall leading to the locker room. "Right here," he said. "Easy to spot because the height is off. It's not even with the other stacks."

"Whose job is it to make sure these are restacked properly?"

"Wendel, the janitor. It's one of the last things he does before he locks

up at night. Nobody wants to come in here in the morning with it looking like a war zone. It's unprofessional. It smacks of laziness and dirt and I want to maintain a well-oiled place. The neatness calms me down."

"Calms you down?" The inspector looked at the man. "From what?"

"From taking a drink. I've been a "Friend of Bill" for fourteen years and this helps me stay centered in a very small way." John looked at the man dead in the eye, not embarrassed, but his face got a little red. "Don't mean to get all "Motorcycle Maintenance" on you; it's what makes this place from becoming just another sweat stained men's club."

"Thank you for your confidence, Mr. Parker. My dad has a drinking problem, a massive one, actually, but he doesn't have the courage to do what you've done."

After eight years on the job, the detective knew that suspects and witnesses and anyone else involved in a case were not black and white. This wasn't "Mannix" or "Barnaby Jones" where scripted stereotypes were what a television audience watched. Humanity was a broad swatch of personalities; some felt like they were the star of their own movie and spouted monologues when he questioned them, others mumbled one-word answers and hoped he go away.

The photographer had long left. Fingerprints were minimal, MacNeil asked the guy to do all the doors and the toilets and the other shower stall knowing there wouldn't be anything conclusive. "The crime scene was a wash," the expert grunted when he packed up not realizing the sick humor of his words.

MacNeil had heard about this gym from the men at work. None of them used the place except for the new duty patrol, this twenty-two-year-old tough boy named Kurtz from Wildwood who couldn't wait to bust someone, a thief, a drunk beach goer, hell, a seventeen-year-old punk who worked the arcade. His ego was enormous and MacNeil warned the Chief of Police that that type of aggression would only lead to bad press and bad public relations.

But MacNeil had planned on coming in here next week and joining up. He missed working out on a regular basis; he predicted that his time for laps in the ocean, jogs on the beach and a few push-ups in the sand weren't going to be enough. He slapped himself mentally at his lack of empathy. *A man was dead. Pay attention!*

The two men returned to the front area. "I want a list of all the members of your gym, their phone numbers and addresses. Can you do that? Also, do you have Alex Kearney's job application?"

John Parker turned instinctively for Gwen. "Yes, I can do that. We have a typed-up list, and I think it's in the office. Gwen will know."

He followed John back to the inner room where Gwen was sitting, talking to Pete Ricca. He stood up when MacNeil entered and tried to look like he had important information to reveal.

"Can you get Detective MacNeil a list of all our members, Gwen, with their phone numbers and addresses? Do we still have Alex's job application?"

Gwen turned to the file cabinet which with a special key on her chain, she unlocked. It was a very organized file cabinet and within a few flips of cardboard, she pulled out two copies and handed them to the detective.

"We have 68 year-round members," she said. "The tourists who drop in for a week and rarely come back, well, until the next summer, that's on a   different list. You want that?"

"I'll take it all, Mrs. Parker, thank you."

Gwen reached further back, retrieved three papers, then squatted to a lower file, rummaged again, and pulled out the job application and resume. Her filing system, it seemed, was impeccable. "This is Alex's," she said.

He gestured to Sgt Ricca to wait outside. "This is now an official crime scene, Mr. and Mrs. Parker, so I'm going to ask you to leave and to give me your keys to the front door. I'm sorry, the gym will be closed for a few days. When it's clear that we won't have to investigate in here anymore, I'll contact you and give the keys back."

"We have an extra set," said Gwen and stopped herself from feeling obstinate. "I'm not trying to be annoying."

"You're not," the detective said. "Just don't come back until I give you the green light. Hopefully it won't be but a few days, so hang tight." He motioned for them to leave and Gwen picked up her jacket and purse. "I'm sorry this had to happen in your place." He almost added, "You seem like good people," but stopped himself because his years of experience taught him the 'nicest' people could rip you off without ever changing their smile.

The Parkers left and Chris MacNeil locked the gym door. The neighbors had already gotten bored and the press had gone back to their desks for copy. The crime tape surrounded the area and he and Ricca tied the yellow rope across the gym's driveway and tied another rope in an "X" across the main door. He gave Pete Ricca half of the membership names and told him to start contacting them, immediately.

"In person?"

"Yes. I want you to see their face, watch their eyes. People who know something can never hide it; it's in the eyes, look where their eyes land. Ask them if they know about the murder, if they knew Alex Kearney, ever worked with Alex as a professional trainer, what they thought of him, and also, where the hell they were last night between 10PM and midnight.

"There are only four people who have a key to the gym: John and Gwen Parker, Wendell, and Alex. When I searched

Alex's pants this morning, all I found was his car keys and this key which I'm betting is his apartment or a house key. So, where is his gym key?"

Sargent Ricca reflexively looked behind him thinking, hoping another officer was here to share the work, but MacNeil stared only at him. "There's nobody else, Pete, except Kurtz who the Chief will loan me for a few hours a day, I'll tell him to interview the neighbors." The Sargent looked overwhelmed.

"That's the downside of working in a small-town, Sargent. Keep at it. You grew up here, you know these people better than I do. But don't assume just because you sat behind some guy you trusted in Biology class in high school means he's off the hook. A lot changes since then, you hear me?"

"Yes, sir," Ricca mumbled.

"You represent the police now, this ain't the prom and this ain't guys night out at Sid's Bar. If you get any guff, give it right back. I'm relying on you, Pete."

Pete Ricca left in the squad car and MacNeil walked down Stockton Place looking at how a murderer could enter or exit the gym without being seen. It was pretty simple, he surmised. Demolished houses were in the same block, large piles of lumber and brick that was waiting to be cleaned up. A few neighbor houses, small, insignificant, were opposite gym but not directly opposite, down toward the end of the block. It's possible someone might have seen a car or heard a car or god, saw a person sneaking around. This would be good for Kurtz. Local boy could also put people at their ease, hell, most of them probably knew him all their lives. If he picked up on anything, they'd trust him enough to be open. Kurtz flew off the handle, but he could uncoil that smile like a snake charmer, and the bulging muscles in his chest when wearing a uniform seemed to do the trick as well.

Seeing something accurate would be miraculous, though it rarely happens. Most witnesses *think* they saw someone or something only so they can be a big wig in the papers, but most of the time, they saw nothing. A crashing tree limb became a car motor starting up, a shadow of a cat became a six-foot man with a limp. It was ridiculous what people wanted to believe, but sometimes, *sometimes*, MacNeil hit paydirt and a witness's testimony broke the case.

MacNeil saw Alex's Chevy Vega parked a block and a half away. Seemed almost intentional, but maybe the street was crowded last night. MacNeil wondered if Mrs. Parker had noticed the car when she came in this morning. He'd have to ask her and find out from which direction she usually arrived.

He circled the car. It had been recently washed; the tires were new and spotless. The sunlight hit the paint and made it a bull attracting red that could be seen half a mile away. No spring mud or winter rust. He felt someone's eyes on him, and he did a quick turn to the left and saw a curtain fall back into place.

He took out his gloves and retrieved Alex's keys from their protective envelope and unlocked the door. The car was empty, neat, clean, to the point that perhaps Alex washed it in order to hide something. Nothing under the seats. Not a wrapper, not an old newspaper, no old clothes or a smelly set of sneakers. He opened the trunk. It had a spare and a jack. Nothing else. MacNeil checked the glove compartment, with only a black inner lining starting back at him. He popped the hood. Again, nothing out of place. The battery had been cleared of accumulated acid battery gunk; the air filter was recently replaced. MacNeil locked up the car, made some notes in his notebook and continued walking then banged a left on Kearney. The irony did not escape him. He sidewinded his way to Hughes St. The detective of Cape May pondered the meaning of that perfect, untouchable car as he walked through the neighborhoods to the Oceanview Restaurant.

It was 8:30 in the morning, the traffic was non-existent in the small grids of Cape May. The silence was indeed golden and he smelled the salt and sea coming from the east. Death among this beauty. He had his share of malice and crime and pure evil in Buck's County, but the vibration of it, this invasion of it in such a beautiful setting was jarring. After his first murder in New Hope, a young actor had been stabbed multiple times then dumped into the canal, MacNeil had a difficult time separating the facts from his disgust. He got angry easily at suspects, threw one man against a wall, lost sleep, trying unsuccessfully to keep the cold detachment of the crime from invading his subjective feelings. His own chief sat him down one day when the tension was becoming unbearable.

"MacNeil, do you want to be a detective or not?" Point blank stare, bottom line question.

"Yes, sir. But-"

"'But' doesn't work. It's either yes or no. It's a profession that a lot of people aren't cut out for. You got the goods, you got the smarts, but I don't want to have to pick some suspect off a sidewalk because you can't control your emotions."

He was turning into his father, he thought. His mother died when he was twelve, and his father became a different man. Gregarious with his poker friends and bowling team, but silent and taciturn at home. Breakfasts eaten in pure silence, the radio a distraction. But when the flare up began, Chris knew it was aimed at him.

"Christ, *walk* to baseball practice, what are you, a flake?"

"Borrow the car? You better fill the tank when you're done."

The bottle already opening, the sound of gold liquid in a glass. "Maybe your mother would have put up with your fucking attitude, but I'm not."

His father's blasts were unpredictable, and his trust at following through on a ride, a dollar, a phone call, even showing up at his high school baseball games was a crap shoot. Biddeford, Maine, where people noticed the bruises, the shame, the flinch during a fun-loving jostle by a coach, all witnessed, but never mentioned. People didn't pry in Biddeford, nobody interfered, not his teachers, not his friends' dads, no one. He too knew how to keep the secrets especially when he came down for breakfast or home from practice and his father grabbed his arm and swung him hard against the kitchen wall. "Talk to me, you little shit!"

He got a job during the summers baling hay for a large milking farm and stayed with it until he graduated college. A couple of the older men, guys in their 20's, muscled and tan and looking like they had it all together yet seeing their future in cow shit, shrugged at his allusions to his home life. They'd seen it themselves. One of the workers had put up an old dilapidated punching bag in one corner of the barn where the men sat around between milking and haying. He filled it back to its normal size with straw and they took turns practicing moves, throwing out punches, actually talking which to Chris, seemed an odd way to connect. But one day when no one was looking, he nailed the sucker, slamming it hard, not letting up, sweating, swearing, crying almost. "You son of a bitch! You fucking asshole!" getting louder and louder until one man smoking outside, heard his yelling and walked in, got closer to put himself in Chris' sight line. Chris stopped and looked over, the man's shadow covering Chris' face, in hindsight, the darkness seemed almost prophetic.

"We all have one of those," the man said nodding at the personified punching bag. "It's better to get it out then living with it."

Chris nodded, breathing hard, holding the bag still.

"Don't let me stop you," the man advised, "just be careful with your wrists. You break those and you're out of a job for the summer." He got a bottle of milk and a sandwich from the refrigerator and left.

Chris MacNeil, years later, remembered that talk, and others that followed until he learned to keep the anger at bay. Empathy, yes, but anger and blowups, and seeing red when no buttons were being pushed made it difficult at times to justify his ability to solve crimes. His boss in Buck's County disagreed.

"Evil is everywhere, MacNeil. If it's in your soul to do this work, you do it. There's no place on earth where you can escape human nature and their capacity for death. Rich, poor, sea, mountains, the city, the slums, the farm, the burbs, it doesn't fucking matter, MacNeil," his supervisor said. "People kill."

Chapter 7

I remember, Kip, when they converted part of Washington Street into a pedestrian mall. 1971. I was 23, just out of Grad school, living in NYC, visiting my parents on Idaho Street, watching buildings get torn down and the road widened and everyone talking like it was going to be the next Main Street, Disneyland. There were protests, I remember that. Whole neighborhoods destroyed that made people wonder if the entire town was going to be exterminated. New side streets created that were like little alleys and byways. Joni Mitchell sang and you knew it was coming: the large parking lot by the Acme.

It didn't matter much to me, Kip. I had New York. Straight out of Colombia and feeling life unfold before me: clubs, parties, friends, sex, showing up for work on time and feeling fine. I could do this forever I told a colleague as I munched on numbers and files and accounts and transactions and watching the money and bonuses flow in. A fast impromptu trip out to Fire Island for three days, a train back to the Village. Isn't this what everyone talked about? Theater and concerts and more friends and more sex and more art galleries and upscale discussions about Ginsburg and Mailer and classic literature and yes,

*it was a wild ride and looking back on it now, it seems more like a 21st
century montage of what a young movie producer envisions Manhattan
in that decade: shot after shot of people and streets and buildings and
subways, spotless, sanitized, and perfectly arranged. None of it true.*

*It's like when I see a movie set in the 1960's and all the extras are
wearing fresh laundered, color coordinated bell bottoms and fringe vests
and oh so kooky wide hats. Christ, that wasn't it at all, nothing like it:
it was hand me downs and holes and body odor and dirty feet and no one
taking responsibility for anything except when to get high.*

*The 70's can be whitewashed as well. And we both know, Kip, it
wasn't. Graffiti art dirtied subway trains and piss and garbage strikes,
when hot nights turned into hangovers and unshaven faces and 25
becomes 26 and then 27 and a boss looking at me with a slight frown
which turns into disapproval which makes me realize the handwriting
could, just could be, on the wall.*

And then it is.

*Ironically, nowadays there is this new, trendy uprise in recording
oral history. Young gay men coming around with cameras and mikes
wanting to do their grad student film on the 70's using first person
accounts. Three of us did comply and they gave us gas fare to drive up
to the Village where they were shooting. I took the bus.*

*It wasn't a grad film project this time, but a more intense
documentary on the Gay Movement (those capital letters, Kip, always
crack me up). We sat on stools in front of a special-colored cloth drop,
sharing stories about New York. They asked us to bring a photograph
of what we looked like 'back then'. We held up our pictures one at a
time. It reminded me of headshots and "A Chorus Line." But I think*

the idea was to show people how ageism is so toxic. I presented the one I have of my standing outside Life Cafeteria in Sheridan Square. I'm 22, shirt unbuttoned down to just above my navel, tight jeans, that thick moustache everyone wanted to kiss. I was cocky and hot and thought I had seen it all. We never saw it all. We never even saw it coming.

One of the guys looked at his shirtless beefcake pose and said with complete resolution and peace, "That's not who I am anymore."

The shoot took all day, we broke for lunch. There was so much footage and I wondered how they would edit it. I said to them, "Don't make us look foolish. We were young, perhaps naïve, but we were there."

Chapter 8

MacNeil sat at the counter of the Oceanview Restaurant eating Eggs Benedict, an eyebrow raised from the waitress who looked like one of those tanned smokers who sat in the sun all summer. After they turned 40, when they laughed, they developed that loud, smoker bray.

But MacNeil didn't give a shit. He had his case notebook that he kept with him, Alex's job application. His address was the same as on his license. Born October 2, 1952, made him 24 years old. MacNeil shook his head, *Jesus, so damn young*. He scanned the application. His high school was in Scriba, NY. Graduated June 1970.

Previous employment was at a gym in Oswego, NY 1974-76.

Three gap years.

Nothing mentioned about a college. MacNeil flipped the paper over: Military History: Coast Guard 3 years: 1971-1974. Stationed in Ketchikan, Alaska.

Additional skills: Electrician. Weight Training Certification USCG

References: Jim Crane in Oswego, NY and a local man: Ray Dieter, Leader of Boy Scout Troop 245, Cape May, NJ.

MacNeil made the notes in his book.

MacNeil made another note: girlfriend (s)?

He tackled the list of gym members and started making associations. Jesus, sixty-eight members, he had thirty-four. Surely there was a way to cut this down. He gestured for more coffee and the waitress got a sense of his importance when she saw his gun in its holster and the peek of a badge inside his coat. She poured her coffee from two feet away as if he was about to lash out and grab her.

"You here on a case?" she asked, snapping her gum as if she were auditioning for a film noir role.

"Yep, and I live here." He dropped the easy stereotypes. "My name's Chris MacNeil, I'm the new detective, started last week."

"I didn't know the cops even had a detective. Isn't this town too small for you?"

"You'd be surprised. I cover the whole county, not just Cape May."

She checked herself. "I'm Lucy Green."

"Pleased to meet you." He smiled.

"You're awfully cute for a detective."

"Well, we have to be, they won't let you graduate if you're not."

Lucy laughed and leaned in.

Christ, why was he flirting? You can get more flies…

"I have a question for you."

"Shoot." Lucy winced. "I didn't mean that."

"Do you know a guy named Alex, Alex Kearney?"

"Lucy, Jesus, Pick up!" The cook from the kitchen window gave her a cold stare while tapping on the counter. MacNeil imagined screaming, like the out of left field explosions his father threw when he was a boy.

"Be right back, hon."

Lucy stacked six plates on her arm like she worked in a circus, and ballet-ed her way to two booths, darting around pouring refills, getting butter, dropping off a check. Chris MacNeil stopped watching. He could talk to her later.

"Alex Kearney?" She said by his elbow. Her voice dropped. "Yeah, I know Alex. Kind of. He's comes in here once in a while. Good looking guy, about my age. He's a big flirt, I gotta say. He's got a smile like a million bucks and muscles," she whistled, "he's always wearing t-shirts or else a shirt buttoned down to here," she pointed to her navel.

"Do you know him well?"

She winked. "You mean, 'did I ever sleep with him?' Nah, but I'd like to. Ya know, a friend of mine slept with him and she said he wasn't very good! Jesus!" Lucy's face imitated the surprise. "Yeah, she said it was over really fast. He didn't pay much attention to her, slam, slam, a few more groans, and then done. Out the door. I told her, 'Hey, he's young, he hasn't learned how to love a woman.' And she said, 'Honey, I had better lays in high school.'"

"All Alex sees is Alex." Lucy shrugged. "So, I stopped making the moves on him after that." She sighed. "But I sure would love to have a try." She remembered the badge and put two and two together. "Is he in trouble?"

"No," MacNeil said. "Not that I know of. Do you know if Alex is a Boy Scout Leader?"

"*Lucy*! Christ, Jesus, Pick up! Get your butt over here!"

The waitress was unfazed. "I think he likes me." She smiled and winked as if to say, *aren't men ridiculous?* She took out MacNeil's check and wrote in big letters: COMP and stuffed it in her apron. "On the house, detective. See you around."

The detective left $5, ludicrous, but worth the info she gave. The boy scout was lousy in bed. Not surprised. He headed out the door and changed gears. The membership men would wait. He wanted to take a look into Alex Kearney's apartment.

Chapter 9

8 Oregon Avenue was a dead-end street in a blue-collar section of The Villas. A town with one main street, the offshoot streets tended to be named after states. The house was on the left, the last house, and it was a neat looking place, well painted, the lawn clean and ready for spring. There were no toys or swings outside. A blue Honda was in the driveway. MacNeil walked to the front door and immediately a man in his 60's opened it. He was as neat as his yard, opened face. "Can I help you?" he offered.

Chris MacNeil showed his credentials and the man's face changed. "Am I in trouble?"

"No, sir, you're not. Does Alex Kearney live here?" he asked.

"Yes, well, not in *here*," he gestured inside the house. "He rents the garage apartment out back." He motioned to the left where, when MacNeil moved back and looked where the man's finger pointed, he saw the small curtained hideaway above the garage. It was painted yellow and the stairs on the outside climbed up presumedly to a door on the far right side. "His car's not here, I guess he didn't come home last night, or he got up really early. I don't pay much attention to his coming and going."

"Does that happen a lot?" MacNeil asked.

"Does what happen a lot?"

"Him not coming home at night."

"Like I said, Detective, I don't snoop on my renters, I don't know what Alex's private life is like."

MacNeil backed up, mentally. Changed gears. *Give him the smile, no need to be obnoxious.*

"Was Alex a good tenant? Did he pay his rent on time, no loud music, no wild parties?"

"Yeah, he is. He's really polite, and when I can't lift something, he'll come in and help me. He's a big guy, he used to be in the Coast Guard and now he works at the gym in Cape May." The man stopped. "You said, *was.*"

"Alex died this morning, sir. He was murdered. We found his body at the gym."

"Christ." He doubled over for a minute and his face was white. Chris thought the man was going to faint.

"Do you want to sit down?"

The man sat on his doorway, leaving the door open and breathed in the cooler May air. He put his head between his legs. "Give me a sec."

MacNeil watched the man, and wondered if he should call for an ambulance. After a minute, the man recovered, sat up and leaned against the door frame. He looked up at MacNeil who instinctively squatted down to meet his gaze.

"How long was Alex a tenant?"

The man took a deep breath. "He moved in here, oh, when was it, last year, September first. I took a shine to him, Detective, he was young, wanted to start a new life, so he said, and liked the quiet and privacy back here."

"Start a new life, how?"

"He didn't elaborate. I think all young men make mistakes or go down the wrong road now and then, I know I did, Detective, I'm sure you did, too. He told me he had a good steady job at the gym which I verified with a phone call; he didn't mention anything about breaking the law, (but then, why would he?) and I wanted to give him a leg up."

"Did he bring people over, or was he ever shouting at someone, say on the phone?"

"Not that I'm aware of, Detective, but really, with the garage being over there, I purposefully didn't keep tabs on him. I wanted him to feel his privacy." The man got a bit teary-eyed. "He was a good kid, Detective. A couple of times, in the winter, I'd invite him over here for supper. He talked about himself, I don't know, stuff that men talk about, nothing too deep, but I called Alex "The Seeker" one night. He smiled at that. I said, 'Alex, your whole life will always be about seeking, and when that desire stops, you'll know you're dead.'"

Chris MacNeil touched the man's arm in a friendly grasp. They were so quiet, a couple of robins swooped near them, landed on the ground, cocking their heads listening for the worms.

"So, Mr. ----"

"Small, Ted Small.

"Mr. Small, do you know of anybody who would want to kill Alex?"

The older man looked at MacNeil with a shocked, frozen face. The question was so out of his realm of reality all he could do was shake his head 'No'.

MacNeil stood up and dug into his pants' pocket. He held up Alex's key chain. "Does this key go to his apartment?

The man stayed mute. He shook his head 'yes'.

"I want to look inside. There might be a clue or something to explain his death." MacNeil looked at the pained sad expression of the landlord and his face melted. *This is the part of my job I never like, never, never, never.*

The older man stayed on the stoop of his doorway and merely nodded. MacNeil turned toward the apartment, saw the tire tracks, only one car. He mounted the steps in the shape of an "L". There were eleven of them. The sadness hit him for a minute, the idea of this young man climbing these stairs every night, perhaps to find relief, seeking his own inner sense of who he was in this make shift womb, climbing these stairs on drunk nights, on sober nights, perhaps with a trick, happy nights, sad nights, lonely nights, and ending up in a shower stall, violently murdered. MacNeil remembered the crushed testicles.

Something in his head started to click.

Chapter 10

Remember skinny-dipping in the Villas, Kip? Those dark nights, no moon, the streetlights were not as prevalent then. You'd be so wrapped up in your own cocoon that you had to break out. You'd say, "Meet me at the bay." and I would, I knew what spot you were talking about. The same beach, the one with the horseshoe crabs, the beach with no people. Rarely. Back then nobody, especially in Jersey, cared about nudity. The two of us chucking it all and running in, you'd like to yell and howl and if anyone heard you, they figured it's just another person jumping in the water. The wild release of it all. You were stronger then, and in the water, you could wrap your arms around my waist, haul me out, and throw me a good three, four feet.

I'd fly through the air and for that one moment, it was all fine. The surge of energy and life force and all those 21st century buzz words people throw around now were what was happening. It was glorious.

The stars, when they were out, were so damn clear. We would lay on the beach looking at them, our bodies dripping wet, no one thought about towels. Half sand, half salt water, we'd lay there and I'd show *you Aquarius and Sagittarius. You'd always interrupt and say, "How do you spell 'Sagittarius'?" because you knew I couldn't.*

When it was later in the summer, September even, we could see Andromeda and her Galaxy, and Pegasus and Perseus, and you became like a little kid, listening to the stories and myths. The things that went on before us. Up there, in the sky. And now, Kip, you're up there in the sky.

Your own myth.

Chapter 11

Detective MacNeil unlocked an unusually bright green door and instinctively drew his gun. He eased forward slowly, all his cautionary skills and training kicking in. *Really? At this dead-end street in the Villas? Danger? Gunshots?*

His by-the-book training ignited automatically. He pushed on the door, easy, easy, ears cocked for a noise, a gasp, a sleeping person calling out, "Alex" and then surprised, screaming at a stranger with a gun.

Silence. The late morning light came in through the door and the side window illuminated an unexpectedly clean kitchen. Dishes washed and put away. No visible food, crumbs, dirty knife, or a crushed can of beer. The small table was spotless except for his latest paycheck from the gym. The kitchen melded into a living room and beyond that a door to a bedroom and another door to the bathroom. One way in and one way out.

The living room was simple and orderly. A couch, coffee table, three plants on the shelf by the two large windows, a cheap television with rabbit ears. A *TIME* magazine was on the coffee table and the place was devoid of sneakers or pants or an old t-shirt thrown anywhere. The boy scout was extremely conscientious. A shag plant hanger hung in the corner with a large spider plant bounding down. The walls were painted a mild blue, five candles in various sizes adorned the room. No ashtrays, no cigarettes, no smelly towels. A green telephone hung on the wall.

On the shelf near the television, MacNeil found two photos of Alex that were unmistakable. The first was Alex with three other men, all shirtless, arms together, Coast Guard haircuts and stupid, drunk smiles. Behind them was an ocean and the beach light seemed hot, sunbaked. Alex looked around nineteen and skinny as a weasel. It almost seemed like he could have been mistaken, maybe one of the other men was Alex. But when MacNeil compared it with the other photo, he knew he saw the same man. This one showed Alex, around 21, beefier, stronger, with a different, older man. They leaned into each other and Alex had his arm on the man's shoulder. The family resemblance was striking. It was either Alex's father or an uncle. But it was Alex, to be sure. The smile that had melt a million hearts; that 'aw shucks' grin which MacNeil confirmed got him clients at the gym. He was the Everyman's friend. When he had his full attention on you, the charm, the light in his eyes must have made his gym clients feel like they were getting their money and body's worth.

Alex Kearney. *I'm sorry you had to die like that.*

The detective took the new picture of Alex out of the frame and put it in his coat pocket.

The bathroom had the same cleaned atmosphere. The shower wore a ring, but otherwise, everything else was spotless. No hairs in the sink, no discarded toilet paper on the floor. It was the Coast Guard discipline.

MacNeil entered the bedroom. The window shades were down which made the room feel like a den, a sexual den of a bachelor who was used to 'entertaining' the ladies, the waitresses of Cape May, the store clerk, hell, maybe even Gwen Parker. He turned on the light.

The bed was made. The room smelled a little bit what MacNeil called "the man smell": sweat and sperm and sheets that could use washing. Again, no old ratty socks, no jockstrap, no god-awful work-out clothes that reeked. It was almost, except for the smell, too perfect. Military training.

MacNeil looked in the closet, the simple, sparse, practical shirts and sweatshirts and two pairs of slacks were hung up neatly. Two pairs of shoes. His dresser drawers were the same, underwear, socks, t-shirts, shorts, work out shorts, bathing suit, everything pristinely folded. Near the socks was a box of condoms. Opened. In a box of twelve, three were missing.

MacNeil looked around, shaking his head at the lack of evidence, unless this neatness, this diligence to order, *was* the evidence. He caught himself scratching his head like some bad TV actor and forced himself to focus. He'd check Alex's phone records later. Alex's wallet didn't have a credit card, he recalled. No photos of women, no ripped pieces of papers or matchbooks with a phone number scribbled on it.

Jesus, Alex. Who were you?

To Chris MacNeil, Alex seemed like a young man making his way, sowing his oats in an easy beach town, just like millions of other young men and women, in the cities, in a school, in a factory, or the army, or whatever scene they were into.

He stood by the double bed and looked again. He felt around the mattress, under the two pillows, feeling for a lump or a gun, or an envelope or bags of dope, something.

He knelt down, looked under the bed, and hit paydirt when he saw the porn magazines.

Chapter 12

There were four magazines in total: two were older, the papers more worn, the cover half ripped off, the other two looked more recent. The pages were shinier, and less handled, but all four magazines were not high-quality publications. The pages were glossy and the paper was thin and cheap. The magazines had indecipherably rationale names like "Genesis", "Cheri", "High Society" and "Man to Man"; magazines MacNeil remotely recognized. He wasn't surprised at what he found; he would have been more surprised if there hadn't been anything to look at for lonelier nights. It was the quality of the photographs that disturbed him: the seedy, crappy pictures from cheaply made movies. Producers fed these rags a pile of stills to promote their latest films.

MacNeil sat on the bed and thumbed through the first one and stopped at what he saw. He pulled out the second one and flipped through until he saw the same thing. Then the third and the fourth. All had a common theme: pictures of Alex.

Different movies, different sets, different 'plots' with different women. In one Alex is wearing a plumbing outfit that, as each photo unfolds, reveals less and less of what he's wearing until he is nude, getting blown, then finally, the big fuck and the money shot. And big it was. MacNeil remembered how Alex looked dead, it was such a sickening comparison, but here, Alex is healthy, and gifted with a large dick, huge balls, and a pounding set of muscles. His hair wasn't the same as the photos on his shelf, it had more grease, or gel that made him look wilder, more the proverbial bad boy that most men who bought the magazine would project themselves onto.

His all-American smile was the same as the photographs in his home, and his face turned to pure lust when he performed. The camera ate him up. He was extremely photogenic.

The detective read the captions and the small promotion for the movies. Each movie had those laughable titles, "Blue Collar Baller" and "While my Husband is Away" were two. The women had different names, but Alex's never changed. Billed as 'Brick Harden', there wasn't anything else mentioned about him. The women were the highlight and the men were the studs brought in to do their job, get paid, and that was it. Buyers of this content didn't have any interest (or did they?) in the male models.

He carried the magazines out to his car, and put them in a plastic bag for fingerprint checks. MacNeil knocked on the front door again, explained to the man the necessity of allowing no one to go into the apartment, including himself. It was a crime scene and MacNeil said he wanted the apartment left locked.

"If I want to call you, sir, how do I reach you?"

The man was still in shock, and mumbled out his phone number. MacNeil wrote it down in his book. "Thank you, Mr. Small, again, I'm sorry this is so distressing. If anything comes to mind, maybe you remember someone coming over late at night, or a fight, or Alex leaving in the dead of night, or anything, please call me." He handed him his card. He shook the man's hand and walked to the car. The neighborhood was silent, a few birds. Idyllic even. The lilacs from next door across the street were so strong, MacNeil could smell them from his car. People were by now finishing their house chores, or taking showers to go out, or joining people for lunch, maybe a church meeting or the second shift on a job, all those normal, terribly unimportant things, and Alex Kearney was eternally dead.

Chapter 13

MacNeil knew a murder case can turn cold really quickly. The first few days were crucial and that meant he wouldn't be sitting at home by 6:30 with a glass of wine. He called the station and asked for the name of the Boy Scout Leader of the local troop. There was only one troop in town and the guy's name was Ray Dieter. He's been married for fourteen years, two kids, ages ten and twelve. He was forty-two years old and lived in Cape May. He was also on Alex Kearney's gym client list.

He got the number for the gym Alex worked in in Oswego, the owner was Jim Crane. Chris put a call into that gym, and a voice picked up on the first ring.

"Crane's." A deadpan male voice and in the background, Chris heard clanging of metal and someone grunting obnoxiously.

"Is this the owner, Mr. Crane?"

"Who wants to know?"

"Sir, my name is Detective Chris MacNeil from the Cape May County Police in New Jersey, could I have a minute of your time?"

There was a pause, almost an intake of breath that MacNeil was used to hearing. "What did I do?" the voice asked.

Was the whole world this paranoid?

MacNeil sat at his desk, blank paper in front of him, pen in hand and didn't care about placating everybody in the universe. "Is this the owner, Mr. Crane?"

"Yes, it is. Jim Crane."

"Mr. Crane," he started, "you didn't do anything, I want to ask you some questions about Alex Kearny."

"Oh. Yeah, just a minute."

There was a sound of a hand over the phone speaker, a muffled voice, a sound of a chair moving, footsteps, a closing of a door and the line went dead.

Jesus Christ.

MacNeil called again and Crane picked up on the first ring. "Sorry Detective, I pulled the telephone wire out of its socket. I had to go to my office to hear you."

MacNeil paused. A purposeful pause, trained, to give the other person a detective's sense of authority, didn't want to hear excuses or reasons for delays, he was here on serious business.

"Mr. Crane, how long have you known Alex Kearny?"

"Why? What happened?"

"Mr. Crane, Alex was found dead this morning. I'm verifying his background history. His resume read that he used to work for you, is that correct?"

"Dead? Jesus, what happened?"

"Mr. Crane, I'm not jumping through your egomaniacal hoops, my time is valuable, answer the question, please."

Chris heard the intake of breath. He waited for the onslaught of defensive arguing that occurred frequently when people were scared. MacNeil's manner plus the word 'detective' triggered that.

"Yes, Alex used to work here. It wasn't long. He was a trainer for some of the members."

"Thank you. Did you know that he was in the Coast Guard?"

"Yes, I did. He grew up not far from here, so when he came back, he contacted me about a job."

"Was he skinny when he showed up?"

"Skinny?" MacNeil could hear the voice change. Crane wasn't expecting that.

"Yeah, skinny."

"No, actually, he wasn't. He was pretty solid, must have bulked up in the Coast Guard, I guess. I didn't ask."

"So, he walks in one day and asks for a job as a *trainer* and you just give it to him?"

"Yes, well, sort of." Crane's voice faltered. "He had some papers from the Coast Guard verifying his service and I asked him questions about body muscle and asked him what he would do if a member wanted help with, I don't know, losing your gut, or building up your biceps. I threw him a couple of different scenarios."

"And did he give you a line?"

"No, he was really good. He knew his anatomy and physiology and demonstrated the techniques he would use with the weights. I was impressed." Mr. Crane softened a bit as he remembered. "He was good kid. The members liked him and word got around and more people started signing up with him and then he quit."

"His resume said he worked for you from late '74 to '76, roughly about a year and a half. Is that true?"

"Yeah, I think that's right. He left in July, August, I think. I'd have to check my payroll to be sure if you want the exact dates."

"Did he tell you why he quit?"

"Not directly. I do remember he said, many times, he was unhappy living here, wanted to move around and see the country, he was restless. I wasn't surprised, Detective, Alex had a look sometimes when he was in between clients."

"Whaddya mean, 'look'?"

Crane's voice got softer, almost fatherly. "A far-away look, probably imagining doing something bigger in a different town. Maybe do boxing in Philadelphia or New York. I wasn't surprised when he quit. A month later, I got another guy, not as good as Alex, but he's building a client base and he's a married guy, so I don't think he's going to jump ship anytime soon."

"Did you ever see Alex with a girlfriend?"

"Jesus, Detective, a guy like Alex always had somebody around. But not in here. It's a 'men only' place, but sometimes, there's a local bar across the street, I'd go in there and see him with someone. Alex was always chatting up the ladies. I don't know, but I think he liked to flirt, get laid, and call it done. He's a good-looking man, Detective, he never has to work at that." Crane stopped as the reality of Alex's death hit him again like a 2x4.

"No, I guess he doesn't. Did you ever see him with one woman for a longer time, someone he was dating, someone he'd shoot the breeze with you about on quieter days?" MacNeil was used to jostling memories from people, it was absolutely incredible how, unless he questioned them, they'd stay in a very small memory lane about someone when in reality, they had so many things to say.

"No," Crane started, "I can't say there was – wait a sec, there was a woman, pretty girl, around 20, 21 maybe, that he mentioned. God, I can't remember her name, but I think that lasted about two months, I don't know for sure."

"Did Alex ever talk about marrying her?"

"Nah, nothing like that. He was dating her, then, I guess they broke up. About three months later he moved away. I gave him a good reference to take with him. Later, I heard he got a job at a gym in your neck of the woods, the owner called me, I gave Alex a big green light." MacNeil heard Jim Crane choke up for a minute. "Sorry, Detective, I don't have kids of my own, but I swear, he felt like a son to me."

"He was a nice man, then, would you agree?"

"Yes."

"Did you ever hear of him getting into an argument with a client or a barroom brawl, or maybe somebody complained to you in person about Alex's behavior or personality?"

"No, everybody liked Alex." There was a pause. "Detective, you wouldn't have called me if Alex died naturally. What happened?"

"He was killed in the new gym he works in. Someone smashed his head in with a 35-pound weight."

"God damn," Mr. Crane said. "God, that's unbelievable. Alex." His voice broke again.

MacNeil waited out the silence. "I'm sorry to have to be the one to tell you that, Mr. Crane. It sounded like you and Alex had a good friendship. Do you have a piece of paper? I want to give you my number. If something odd or different or new hits your memory, please let me know. Anything can help in solving this."

He heard Jim Crane open a desk drawer. MacNeil recited his number and he heard the sound of a pencil scratching on paper. "If you lose that, you can call the Cape May Police Dept, they'll find me."

"Thank you, Detective." The anger rose in his voice. "And find the fucker who did this." He hung up.

Chapter 14

2:00 PM. MacNeil sat in his office with Sgts Kurtz and Ricca. Three slices of warm pizza lay in a box and he picked one and offered the other two to his partners. Ricca, a bit fussy about getting grease on his uniform, passed, but Kurtz's paw snarfed up one and then the other, smacking his lips and making unapologetic gulping noises.

"Jesus, Kurtz, stop smacking! Makes my stomach churn!" MacNeil barked.

"Sorry, Detective" Kurtz mumbled, wiped his hands on his pants and pushed over a sheet. "This is what I got from the neighbors."

He had made a column of names and phone numbers and next to that, a brief summary of what they saw or heard. It was actually quite organized, neat, strong, legible handwriting. MacNeil hadn't worked this closely before with the new man, but he shook his head in gratitude. "Nice job, Kurtz, somebody trained you well!"

MacNeil was the type of man who didn't want a lot of superfluous details when it wasn't necessary. He knew if there had been a neighbor with a strong lead, Kurtz would have singled that out, or drawn an asterisk next to the name, something to let MacNeil know the rest of the information might not be that worthwhile.

And sadly, it wasn't. Witnesses were all over the place. They saw a woman slink by wearing a large black hat, who then stopped and lit a cigarette, a car pulled up to the curb with three people in it, all acting furtively, then the car pulled out. No one had gotten out of the car. Another saw two men walk by, carrying beer cans. One heard glass smashing, like a window or a windshield, another heard a gunshot, another person heard a scream.

"God almighty," MacNeil groaned, "this is pretty useless, Kurtz."

"I know, sir, I talked to everyone on the street and to be honest, I don't think any of them were awake after 10:00. The janitor left the place at 9:30, right?"

"Yep, according to John Parker, Wendell's shift ended at that time every night. He went out the main door, locked up, and I guess walked home. I'm interviewing him after this."

"Maybe Wendell was running drugs."

"Could be, but John Parker closes the gym for good at 8 PM. Everyone is gone. Wendell comes in at 8:15, John leaves and locks Wendell inside. Wendell cleans, and then Wendell leaves and locks the door behind him. So, I guess Wendell could unlock the door to let someone inside or do a drug run, or sell dope to someone inside the door frame, but Alex was there, so he wouldn't be that stupid."

"Unless he's selling them to Alex."

Ricca popped up, "So, how many people had a key to the place?"

"Four. John and Gwen Parker, Wendell, and Alex. The key was for the front door. The back door was always locked and John alone had that key. He never uses it. He does only if he has to bring in something he bought, like a new bench, or weights or anything else that's bulky. According to him, he hasn't done that, but I'll check his purchase orders."

"But Alex didn't have his key in his pants pocket, right?"

"Yes, Ricca, that's right."

"So whoever killed him took the key, in order to lock the door behind him."

"It seems that would be logical."

"Christ, that could be anyone!" Ricca wasn't very experienced as a cop, but had a terrific love of puzzles and math problems. It was an undiscovered gift that allowed him to think outside the box, to see a problem from more than one side. He hadn't had many opportunities to use this gift, but MacNeil smiled to himself when he saw the wheels turning.

"Alex's phone records turn up nothing out of the ordinary," MacNeil reported. "Local calls, calls to his father, nothing else." He moved to a new topic. "How far did you get on the client list, Sgt?" MacNeil asked gesturing to Ricca and his pile of papers. Unlike Kurtz, Ricca tended to take too many notes, writing down answers to even the most useless facts, but facts were always facts, and he felt that the answer to any problem could be found in the most unlikely of information.

"I got through 50% of them. Most of these men live nearby. They walk to the gym or they drive over after work." He waved his finger through the list, acting like he was about to give a lecture that MacNeil had no time for.

MacNeil waved his hand, "Give it over," he said.

Ricca passed the paper, feeling a bit sheepish in front of Kurtz. The other cop didn't seem to care or notice.

MacNeil skimmed the sheets. "Great work here, Ricca. Anything that you notice? A pattern or an alibi that didn't check out?"

"Alibis were all tight, sir as far as I can tell. These men, the ones who hired the trainer, liked him. They were shocked to hear that he was dead."

"What did they like about him?"

"He didn't waste their time or money. He knew his material; his body was proof of everything he taught them. He was likable. That was the most common word they used. The men I questioned genuinely liked Alex. They asked him questions about their bodies, and didn't feel ashamed at their ignorance. Alex coached them, helped them, gave them encouragement. There was only one thing some of them commented on."

"Really?" MacNeil felt a whiff of hope amid this glossy pat on the back eye-rolling praise. "What's that?"

"Some of them admitted to Alex, at times, being standoffish. He'd show up and do his job, but he wasn't always as friendly as he was the week before, more like something was on his mind, preoccupied, so his camaraderie was somewhat chilled."

"Camaraderie," MacNeil repeated. "They actually said that word?"

"Well, no…" Ricca faltered.

MacNeil sat digesting the information and the false reporting and let the silence grow to be uncomfortable. It made its mark. He sighed, "So, Sgt, did any of them say what Alex was preoccupied with? Did he tell them anything, something about money, or women or men or a situation with his parents or siblings?"

"Not that I know of, sir." The voice was getting small and MacNeil knew he had to keep Ricca from disappearing. *What is this, track practice?*

"Sgt, would you please go back to the men who mentioned the chilled Alex and ask them if he had ever said anything about it to them. You have that genuine, sincere approach, it keeps people off their guard. If you can get any inkling on that, it could help in a big way."

Ricca smiled. "Sure, Detective."

"And finish the rest of your list by tonight."

Kurtz was getting itchy. His hours allotted to working on the case were up and he, MacNeil could see, was anxious

83

to stretch, move, drive around Cape May, hand out parking tickets, cruise by the high school when it let out. MacNeil rolled his eyes. "Kurtz, here," he ripped his own Alex Kearney client list in half and handed it over. "Start on this in the morning, you can get further than I can, and report back to me before noon."

"Sir." He folded up the paper, stuffed it in his pants and left. Didn't tuck the chair in, didn't say goodbye, self-absorbed, already reaching for the cop car keys.

"Get yourself some lunch, Sgt, and then head on out."

"Yes, sir. Thank you." Ricca collected the list, left the detailed papers with MacNeil and walked out. The office was quiet, a phone rang down the hall, the floor was dirty and the windows were grimy. MacNeil made a point to talk to the Chief about some heavy cleaning around here. It was getting depressing, and Alex Kearney was not the kind of ghost that would haunt him, but he did.

A cop from the front desk poked his head in. "Detective?"

"Yes, Officer, what's happening?"

"Wendell Taylor is here. He said Sgt Ricca called him and asked him to come by, but Ricca left. You want to see him?"

Chapter 15

We have the internet now, Kip. It makes finding information, facts, rumors, publicity, the useful and the useless so much easier. It's a matrix that's taking over to the point that half the population doesn't know what's real and what's not. They call it Information Pollution. Anything goes on the Internet and it can be a good tool for so many things, but recently, Kip, I read that middle school kids can't tell the difference. They think the internet is real and that a math teacher standing in front of them asking them to analyze or put two minutes' worth of time into a word problem is a bad dream that will go away. The switch in their brains makes them think that consequences are non-existent, empathy is considered weak and useless, and if anything: a nagging parent, a disgruntled teacher, a bad grade, makes them upset, well, that emotion can be wiped away by a flip on their iPhone.

I'm glad I'm not a teacher. I don't envy the garbage they have to take. Remember the case you had in the school?

I know, Kip, Anne Frank said it best. I sound like a disgruntled old senior, that's what you would have called me, and yes, there is a lot of goodness in the world. In the winter, the boy scout troop spreads out over

Cape May and shovels snow or helps get a cold battery started. Many a winter morning I'm glad to hear their knock on my door. I'm not feeble, Kip, not at all, but a back can only take so much snow drift. Those kids, maybe they feel forced to smile, maybe they roll their eyes at all this civic duty and call it bullshit behind our backs, but I like to think they are genuine. I give the leader money to treat the guys at the Oceanview or Joe's Pizza, whatever makes them happy.

Chapter 16

"Wendell," MacNeil checked his notes, "Taylor, thank you for coming, please sit down."

Wendell wore gray coveralls that extended down to his wrist and ankles, with a garage logo that read Gaebel's plastered on the left side of his chest. MacNeil shook his hand, a hand that was calloused, a strong grip with grease under the fingernails. The man was about 5'10", uncombed, uncontrollable black hair that curled in the back and over his ears. He looked MacNeil in the eye. He dug in his pocket and handed the detective his driver's license.

"What's this for?"

Wendell Taylor didn't mess around. "You gonna ask for ID, so here it is."

"Have a seat, Mr. Taylor." MacNeil read the license. Date of birth: September 12, 1942. Address:13 H Street, West Wildwood. He counted the years. 35. "How long have you lived here, Mr. Taylor?"

"All my life, Detective. Born and raised. I grew up in the house where I live now. My mom is still there with me. My dad died when I was fourteen and I felt like I had to take care of her and my younger brother. He has Down's Syndrome."

So many thoughts went through MacNeil's head. *Grew up in the house where I live now. Pat answer, almost prepared.*

He copied the information in his notebook and handed the license back. "Where do you work?"

"Part time at the gym, and part time at Gaebel's." There was a simplicity to the man, not stupidity, but an honest, what you see is what you get attitude which MacNeil wondered if it was genuine or a laid-back way of not getting involved. He might be like this at work, in a bar, at home, on a vacation. *This guy's definition of a vacation was probably a drive up to Atlantic City.* MacNeil checked himself and adjusted his tie. *Christ, you can be a real snot sometimes.*

"Tell me, Mr. Taylor, what happened last night. Let's start with the gym. What time did you get there?"

Wendell didn't sit back in his chair, didn't relax. He wasn't sweating or stammering, no fidgeting shoes or tapping on his knee. He looked at MacNeil like he was talking to a customer in the garage telling him his two front tires were shot. "I got to the gym at 8PM, that's my regular shift time. John Parker was there, the gym closes at that time so there were maybe," he didn't even look away to speculate, "three, maybe four men left. They were headed out the door, saying 'Good Night,' and John was locking the door up behind them. It's a usual routine."

"Okay, so then…"

"John stayed another fifteen minutes, I don't know, I wasn't paying attention. He was behind the desk, putting memberships and sign-ins in a pile," he shrugged like a teenager not knowing the answer to a geometry problem. "You'd have to ask him for those details."

"I will. So, do you have a routine that you follow every night?"

"Depends."

"Depends on what?"

"Depends on how crowded the day was, how many people came in. But I usually take a quick look around the room and what takes priority. Sometimes it's the weights, sometimes the benches, sometimes it's the locker room."

"But you can't see the locker room from the front desk, how do you know what requires your attention in there?"

"I don't. But I look around and then stroll through the place and make a mental check list of what has to be done. I walk into the locker room as well, even as a back-up to John Parker. Sometimes, there's one stray guy getting dressed who doesn't realize we closed."

"Does that happen often?"

"No. Once in a while."

"Can you be more specific?"

Wendell stared at the detective and MacNeil thought the man was going to say, "What the hell do I look like, a bookie?"

"About once or twice a month," Mr. Taylor responded. "I can't be any more accurate than that."

"Was Alex there?"

"No, he wasn't. He didn't show up until later."

"Alright. So, you arrive. You look around. John is putzing behind the counter. You're checking out the dirtiness factor of the place, would that be accurate to say?"

"Yes."

"Is it possible, Mr. Taylor, for someone to hide out in there, after hours?"

"Did you see the place, Detective?"

MacNeil wasn't used to having his questions answered with a question. "Yes, I did. But you've worked there for two years."

"No, Detective. There's no place to hide that wouldn't be noticed by either John or me or even Gwen."

"When did John leave?"

"He left at 8:15 or so. He locks the door behind him and I start to work."

"Did you notice anything out of place?"

"The whole place is out of place, Detective. That's why they hire me. I'm not trying to be complicated, it's a job, Detective. I clean the place. I start with the messiest part and make sure the whole gym looks good for when Gwen comes in in the morning. If it isn't-"

"If it isn't, then what?"

Wendell Taylor cracked a smile. "Well, Gwen will tell me about it. When I first started, I wasn't very particular about cleaning. Hell, it's a men's gym, detective, these guys won't care if it's not spit and polish. But Gwen did. She'd come in the next day and start making a list of what was wrong, slamming the words like they were punishments, practically breaking through the paper she was so mad, and leaving the note for me when I walked in later."

"Did John tell you as well?"

"Yeah, but not in the same tone. I dig it. Gwen Parker is a businesswoman, and they both pretty much told me, 'You wanna work here or not?'"

"So you improved?"

"Yeah, they pay me well. I like going in there. I have a free membership which I use as much as I can. It's almost like cleaning my own shop. I take pride in that, and you know, I'm not some janitor that gets treated like shit. John knows I'm good with electricity, wiring, plumbing, it saves him a lot of money to pay me to do the job than bring in some stranger. Sometimes, if I see something starting to fall apart, if it's easy, I'll fix it myself and not even tell them."

"So what time did Alex arrive?"

"He came in just before I left. I'm done at 9:30 and he unlocked the door and walked in a few minutes before that."

"He unlocked the door, how?"

"With his key."

"He had his own key. He didn't bang on the door and ask you to let him in?"

"No, he didn't have to bang on it. He had his own key. I was in the locker room and heard the door open, so I poked my head around the corner just to make sure it was him."

"So, he's done this before?"

"Yeah, a few times. Enough for me to not be surprised. He said he liked being alone, working out, not having to talk to anyone."

"Mr. Taylor, I'm confused. Your job is to clean the place, spotless, enough to satisfy Gwen Parker's standards. And then just as you have everything spic and span and about to leave, Alex Kearney would stroll in and work out? Sweat dripping on the benches, weights thrown around?"

"Yeah, it's a little stupid, I agree. But, to be honest, Alex was incredibly conscientious and neat. Gwen and John allowed him to come here after hours, maybe they set up some kind of arrangement with Alex, you know, come in if you want, but no visitors, and clean and put away what you use, and lock the damn door when you leave. You'd have to ask them."

Wendell Taylor showed no signs of impatience. He never looked at his watch, or gave an eye roll or answered in a tone that displayed any kind of resistance to the questions. Again, it reminded MacNeil of a high school kid sitting in the principal's office, being questioned, explaining his point of view, following the rules.

"So, Alex walks in, how did he seem?"

"I don't know what you mean." The first hint of defensiveness.

"Well, was he angry or impatient? Did he seem worried or distracted, maybe he was scared. Was his behavior any different than usual? Did he talk about anything?"

"To be honest, I really didn't notice him. I was hungry and wanted to finish up, and Alex walked in and said, 'Hello, Wendell, what's up?', stuff he says all the time. He didn't talk to me about anything in particular, he was headed to the locker room to change and I was wrapping up the trash and heading out the door. He looked like he usually does, friendly, but ya know," Wendell smiled a second time, "he did seem a little cocky. It's that kind of walk when you know later on that night you're going to get laid."

"Did Alex tell you that?" MacNeil asked.

"No, Detective, he didn't. It's not something you can call a fact, but we all know that look. He had that look."

"So, you left."

"Yes, I left. I yelled 'So long, Alex,' and I heard him yell back from the locker room. I took out the trash and locked the door behind me."

"Are you 100% positive you locked the door? I'm not saying you're incompetent, it's just sometimes, I forget to lock something because I'm thinking about something else. You said you were hungry. Is it possible you raced out of there with a hamburger on your mind?"

"I'm 100% positive I locked the door. I have a habit that I use every night. I lock the door. I even say to myself, 'Wendell, lock the door.' I do it and then I pull on the door three times, hard, so it makes a banging noise. Detective, when I tell you I locked the door, I *locked* the door."

"Did you see anyone standing outside? Maybe someone watching you, waiting for you to leave?"

"No. It's a quiet street at night, Detective. If there had been anyone hiding, true, I might not have seen them, but in my recollection, I checked around the door, and then walked away. My car was parked on Kearney. I got in and drove home."

"What time did you go to work this morning at Gaebel's?"

"I punch in at 10:00. Gaebel is a good man, a good mechanic. He's one of the best."

MacNeil thought of something. "Did you ever use Alex as a trainer when you worked out?"

"A couple of times."

"Was he any good?"

"Actually, Detective, he was very good. He listened. I think that's the biggest factor that made him popular. He listened. He didn't just start telling you what to do like some Drill Sargent. No one wants that shit. He worked with me as I am, the way my body worked. He knew a lot of good tips. He could prioritize what you could work on and made a list of what he saw as important and it was up to me to do the exercising or not. He didn't judge."

"Did you ever work with Alex when he was in a bad mood?"

"A bad mood? I think everybody goes to work sometimes in a bad mood, Detective. He might have been, but he didn't show it. Barking orders or getting testy with me, is that what you mean?"

"However you want to define it."

Taylor's eyebrows went down, as if he were trying to give directions to the stray tourists who occasionally stopped off at Gaebel's clearly lost and seeking his help but at the same time not believing him, practically defying him. The tourist who was so obstinate, so intent on being right, he often snapped, "Then why'd you ask me?" and turned his back and sauntered into the garage to work on a car. "I don't know, Detective. He liked his job. That's the feeling I got."

"Mr. Taylor, you were the last person to see Alex alive. Did you kill him?"

If Taylor was surprised at the jab attack, he showed no sign. "No, Detective," he said, "I didn't."

Chapter 18

Wendell Taylor left and the room felt hot. The smell of sweat and dust and car grease drifted around, down the hallway to the typing sounds hammering out from another room. MacNeil took off his jacket, undid his tie and hung them on his chair. He opened the only window in the office and the spring air hit his nostrils. He smelled churned over dirt and a small bit of lilac. The linoleum floor was dirty, the cigarette smoke from the Chief's office floated in the hall, the windows were getting grimier. He wrote a reminder to discuss an overall cleaning for this two-floored public facility that was looking like a two-bit boxing ring.

The notebook lay open and he spent an hour transcribing his notes, typing his shorthand into cohesive English for the daily report. He worked silently, no radio, no interruptions. He kept his door open but if a cop saw him typing, unless he had to, didn't interrupt him. Even though Chris MacNeil had been on the job for a short three days, most people knew the code of the Detective. It was universal.

4:30. He folded up and pocketed the client list and went out for a walk. Cape May had this evasive ever-present charm that made itself known despite the tear downs, the renovations, the new sights on hotels and tourism. The Victorians were dilapidated, but so much effort was going in to renovate them and bring them to life. "Recalled to Life". He remembered that as a chapter title, but he couldn't remember where.

He went over in his head the statements of Gwen Parker and Wendell Taylor. They had a connection, or was it a secret? He nodded his head to the firemen washing the truck and they didn't really recognize him. "He's the new dick," he heard one of them say. "Don't know much about him."

Della's 5 & 10 was quiet. He headed toward the back and sat on a stool at the end. He ordered coffee from a new woman. He hadn't seen her before, but there were a lot of shop owners and workers he didn't know. He only knew the owner and she wasn't around today. He gestured toward a donut from the tray and she put it on a plate. She seemed bored, but there were only two people in the place. He sat and thought and took facts and twisted them around and wondered who was lying and who was telling the truth. He didn't notice the dark clouds coming in, the drop in temperature; not until the sky opened did he look up.

The Whaler Bookshop was a block and a half down from Della's, and he was soaked when he sprinted in. The door was solid oak, and he surprised himself when it crashed against the side wall and knocked over a stack of books causing the man at the counter to look over. MacNeil closed the door behind him and dripping wet, restacked the books trying not to damage them.

"Thanks," the man said, and MacNeil couldn't tell if it was gratitude or sarcasm.

The list in his pocket's first name was here: Matt Ryan.

"So, this is 18, 19, 20, and 20 is 40 and 10 is 50. Thank you, Mrs. Carey for coming in today. Don't get too wet!"

Mrs. Carey was one of those stereotypical Cape May types who had bought five novels and then paid with a 50-dollar bill. "This is my favorite bookstore, Mr. Ryan, my absolute favorite!"

"Well, it's the *only* bookstore in Cape May County, Mrs. Carey, but you know that already! As always, thank you for your patronage."

Mrs. Carey walked to the door past the wet detective like she was about to present an award, when she unconsciously stopped and looked him up and down. She lingered on his hard nipples pushing against his wet shirt, the wet bulge in his pants, a barely perceptible eyewink of satisfaction, then glided past, already reaching for an umbrella.

"She says that every time she's in here, but she buys books," Matt Ryan flashed a smile. "How can I help you?"

MacNeil stepped closer to the counter, and showed his badge. "I'm Detective Chris MacNeil, from the Cape May County Police, are you Matt Ryan?"

Matt Ryan's look was a bit frightened, perhaps more startled than frightened. He came from around the counter and stood closer to the detective. He was about 29-30 years old, younger than MacNeil expected, dark hair, shaved Irish man-boy face, but a strong 5'11" frame. His shirt was unbuttoned one past normal and his chest was tight. His sleeves were rolled up and his hairy arms and tight biceps were taut against the shirt. His pants were snug, hiding nothing, and MacNeil wondered at the disco look. Was he trying to give off the image of being hip in this small town? A bookstore worker by day and a drug dealer by night?

"Yep, that's me."

MacNeil matched the blue eyes staring at him, and there was a quick look, a break in the eye contact from the bookstore owner, fast, subtle, but undoubtedly, a onceover on his body, especially his chest from the wet shirt.

MacNeil took control. "I wondered if you had a minute, I wanted to ask you some questions." He relished the vagueness of that declarative statement. It worked every time and this was no different. He could read Ryan's mind as it did a quick inventory of his entire life and illegal activities: drugs, drinking and driving, destruction of property, knocking up someone underage, cheating on taxes, cheating on a wife, gambling debt, hiring prostitutes, it all flashes across the eyes until the person gives up in either resignation, surrender, or wide-eyed puzzlement.

"Sure, Detective," he said.

MacNeil reached for the photo of Alex in the jacket he left at the office and punted. "Do you know a man named Alex Kearney?"

Matt Ryan's eyes wandered the store, hoping to see another customer, as he stalled for time, almost as if he were caught in a lie. "Alex Kearney, well I don't know, maybe. I used to live in New York, I knew a lot of men, friends I had, or met at a party or on a vacation, maybe had dinner with. He wasn't a co-worker…." He scanned the shelves, as if he were looking for the author in the "K" section. MacNeil could see, as the clock went by another minute, that Matt Ryan was reaching a point of no return, as if he would say, 'Hell, I give up, I can't stand here all day trying to retrieve a name. What do you want?'

"That name doesn't ring a bell?"

"No, Detective, it doesn't, like I said, I lived in the city for a long time, is this someone I knew from college?"

"He's someone who works at the Cape May Gym."

"Alex!" Matt Ryan's face lit up, mostly out of relief that he didn't have to incriminate some Ecstasy pusher out of the Village from six years ago. "Oh, *that* Alex! Yeah, I know Alex. I didn't know what his last name was." He gave a mischievous smile. "Everybody knows Alex."

"What do you mean by 'know'?"

"He's a popular guy. He works at the gym as a trainer, knows his stuff, good-looking man and he knows it too, likes to show it off. But he has a good heart, if you know what I mean. He seems almost innocent."

Not to the porn world he isn't.

Instead, MacNeil asked, "Did you ever hire him as a trainer?"

"I did, about three times, I think. I'd have to check my bank statements to verify that."

"Was he good at being a trainer?"

Matt Ryan smiled at a memory that made him chuckle. "Oh, yeah, he was good. I worked with him for a few Sundays, he gave me great tips. When I was lifting a weight the wrong way, he was right on it, making sure I had the proper form. He kept me from really doing damage to my back." Ryan unconsciously puffed the chest a little bit more, flexed his arm, expanded his shoulders to show the fruits of his labors. "Did something happen to Alex?"

"He died this morning."

"Jesus! Was it a car accident? Did he drown?"

"He was murdered, Mr. Ryan. I'm here to find out who killed him." Christ, he hated when he sounded like some stereotypical detective, especially in a bookstore full of one-dimensional amateur sleuths and cheesy whodunnits.

"God, I'm sorry to hear that. He was a good man."

"Did you ever notice if Alex got into a fight or an argument?"

"In the gym?"

"At the gym, on the beach, in a bar, some trashy alley. You work here, maybe you heard some gossip or anything, this town is pretty small."

"I don't just work here, Detective, I own the store, just for clarification. And no, I haven't heard anything about Alex except he does get around with the women. I got the feeling he liked having a good time, but no commitments, very Gordon Lightfoot if you know what I mean. But, what the hell, he's young, he's got a lot to offer in the looks department, he likes to flirt. I saw him once in Sid's Bar and he was talking to a woman, older woman, it almost looked like Gwen Parker, but I don't think it was her. I don't know, I don't want to give you false information; he was flirting, but so was she, so big deal."

"Do you know of anyone who might want to kill him? Maybe he was selling drugs, or part of a gambling racket?"

"Not that I know of, Detective. Like I said, he was a typical 20-something horny beach boy well-oiled man who liked to bang the ladies. If he fathered any kids, I didn't know about that."

"Mr. Ryan, where were you last night between 10 and midnight?"

"At home." No sense of plotting or scheming. "I called my sister at 10:15, she lives in California and the rates are a little cheaper. She and I talked for about 90 minutes or so. I remember hanging up around midnight, but my phone records would be able to confirm that."

"Thank you, sir. By the way, did Alex ever come in here?"

"To buy a book?"

"Yeah, what *else* would he be in here for?"

The businessman part of Matt Ryan stepped forward. "He did. If I can recall, he bought a copy of *Dune* once and a copy of *Slaughter House-Five*, sort of odd for a Coastie."

"So, you knew he had been in the Coast Guard?"

"Detective, everybody knew that. It was part of his pitch to get men to hire him at the gym. I think he told me he bulked up and trained there. Apparently, when he first joined up, he was a skinny kid barely able to lift a dime."

"Do you think Alex was a gigolo? On the side?"

Matt Ryan shook his head. "I don't know, Detective. If he was, I never heard about it. I liked him. He was a bit cocky at times, but who isn't at that age. I'm sorry that he's dead. I hope he didn't suffer."

Chris MacNeil saw through the body bravura and the tight clothes. The man seemed genuine although he would check his phone records. "Thank you for your time, Mr. Ryan, if you ever want to go-" he felt the heat of red on his face, and saw the corners of Ryan's mouth rise up briefly, "I mean, if you think of anything that might help with this case, maybe something Alex said, or something you saw," he handed Matt Ryan a card, "please give me a call."

The two men shook hands, and Matt Ryan put the card in his wallet. The detective, all business and concentration, stepped out into the rain and didn't seem to care that he would get wet all over again.

Chapter 19

MacNeil walked to the police station, the rain had stopped half way there. The sun popped out and the sunset left behind hit the upper windows of the Victorians. The town hummed. MacNeil felt it every time he was outside. It wasn't the people or cars or machinery or construction. Cape May had its own vibration, a connection to the ocean. MacNeil laughed and cringed a little inside because if he had told that to anyone on the force, they'd give him those blank, judgmental, 'what are you, a weirdo?' looks which translated to a distancing he couldn't afford at this job.

The fresh air that blew over the ocean and across his back after the rain stopped was a complete 180 degree turn from the stuffy, smoke-filled police station that accosted his nose when he walked through the front door. The waste paper buckets reeked of day-old coffee cups and phlegm. *Christ, clean this dump!* From his office he called the Parkers and asked them to come in to see him tomorrow at 10 AM.

He sat at his desk, and leaned back in the swivel chair. God, he felt insignificant, almost a parody, like something out of "Barney Miller". He made some notes, then called the next four names on his list of gym clients and set up appointments with each one for that evening. He knew during suppertime, those men would be home from work, potentially, and he could talk to them briefly on a porch or in a mud room, somewhere where they would be away from their families or wives or girlfriends or army pals, and he could look them in the eye. The eyes said everything. Every time. He put on his coat with Alex's photo in the side pocket, left the tie and walked home.

MacNeil lived in an apartment on Washington Street, an easy walk from his office. It was not a typical apartment building, more like a funky house broken up into four units: two on the ground floor and two on the top floor. MacNeil's was on the top right. The house, he could see, would be covered in vines and full bushes and flowers in the summer and the staircase leading from the outside walkway swung up in a curve to his front door. The door was part of his balcony overlooking the street and the one bedroom set up inside was well lit and finely balanced. The door led into the living room, which meandered into a kitchen, a small hallway where the bathroom was and then the bedroom which overlooked the back area: a gravel parking lot for four cars. His Chevette Hatchback Coupe was parked, untouched.

He changed his shirt and washed his face, sensing the concentration of the last twelve hours beginning to show. He put on a new tie. He had only eaten a donut so he fried three eggs, wolfed down a piece of toast, found another jacket, transferred the photo and headed out the door.

These four interviews were nearby in this small town, and it felt good to stretch his legs, breathe the salt air. He felt tired, but he knew a drop in focus could cause him to miss an important word, or a gesture, or a look that could be investigated. MacNeil was smart enough to pull off the ruse: act like he's making routine inquiries, but underneath, he was sharp, intense, missing nothing.

They were busts. He planned well, interrupting their dinner to throw them off guard, and taking them outside, out of earshot. He walked them down to the edge of the driveway, not caring if their food got cold. He wanted them alone. He sensed their backs stiffening and one of the men about 6'3" puffed out his body, "What do you want, Detective," he demanded, strutting to the road, making sure he wasn't going to get pushed around.

MacNeil had seen it all, nothing intimidated him. He laughed inside because it was often the one with the puffiest demeanor, the intense macho stare, the standdown like some kid in a high school locker room who ended up crying when he put the cuffs on him.

These men revealed nothing. Even with the photo, three of them had never trained with Alex; two out of those three never even knew the gym had a trainer nor did they recognize him. The fourth man knew Alex, worked with him a few times, liked him. Alex had helped him with some squat formations, gave good advice, an overall good guy, but for him, and for many others, out of sight, out of mind. The gym was an hour spent away from their jobs, their bosses, their wives, like a poker game or bowling, a time to grunt and sweat and get the mojo back, feel young again, or, in many of these men, keep the youth they saw fading in the mirror. Alex was a barely detectable blip on a much bigger life radar screen.

Not expecting much, MacNeil tucked in his notebook, thanked the men for their time and meandered through the streets of Cape May. He stopped into a recent discovery, the King Edward bar in the Chalfonte Hotel. It was its own hideaway, tucked in the back of the building. He avoided the main entrance in the front; instead, he walked outside down the left side of the hotel toward the back, then up the three steps to the intimate porch and a small side door. The bar inside was a little like stepping into a Fitzgerald novel, a narrow room with the dark wood, the low lights, a place for bourbon and no one to bother him. At this hour, there were five men in the place and two women. The two women sat at a small table, but MacNeil sat at the bar. He felt their eyes on him, and he did a quick side glance to see who they were. He caught one looking at him a bit too long, and she unmistakably had done that on purpose. He gave her a nod, but otherwise, turned to the bartender, "Maker's Mark, water back."

Chris MacNeil's career was taking off in a way he didn't expect. Alex Kearney's death by now had been in the papers, with god knows what grainy photo of him at the crime scene this morning. His face would not necessarily be instantly recognizable and MacNeil liked that for now. It allowed him to remain incognito to a degree, feel out of place, feel like an outsider. Or, as he chided himself more realistically, to hell with what people knew or thought, he wanted a drink.

There was a small cloud of fog drifting through the streets, and the bourbon warmed him up. One was his limit because when he spontaneously decided on two, he felt out of his league, out of control, and all he saw was his father's drunk, angry, or worse, indifferent face as it turned on him and in his teen years, hit him. Later, the man ignored him completely while maintaining a certain tinge of disgust at trying to figure out who the hell this kid was and how the hell he helped create this.

"His balls were *crushed*!"

MacNeil tensed, clutched his glass. It was the man five stools away talking to the bartender.

"Jesus!"

"No," the bartender said, "they *would* have been crushed if that line drive had hit him in the nuts. Lucky he's got fast reflexes and his glove grabbed the ball."

"God, that would have been hell," the drinker said, "my cousin got shot there in 'Nam, but, the bullet didn't do any damage. They were able to patch it up, or whatever the hell they do. He's got two kids since then."

"That are *his*?"

The drinker chuckled and handed over a five. "Yeah, they're his." He saddled off the stool. "See you around, Jim."

"Take it easy, Frank."

The light outside was a cool, green, shiny surface with the smells of mud and seeds and growth.

"There's this guy you should meet," the one woman was saying to the other as they stood up and put on their coats. "He's right what you're looking for. He keeps his mouth shut."

"Hey, didya hear they got a new cop in town?" another drinker yelled to the bartender who looked like he didn't realize his job was becoming a stereotype in a bad B movie. Might as well wipe the counter to help create the illusion.

The bartender wanted to say, "You talkin' to me?" in his perfected DeNiro voice. Instead, he said, "Yeah, I heard. He's been here about a month."

A month?

"He's the new county detective, right?"

"God, I don't know, Carol," the other woman giggled on one too many gimlets. "It sounds tempting, but-"

The voice drowned out by a loud thump on the door. It was the wind.

"Yeah, he's from Buck's County, I don't know nothing about him."

"He's a trip, Carol, I'm telling you that. God, it's big enough to make you wonder about the whole species. I'll get you the name, and after that, it's your call." They moved past MacNeil toward the door. "Trust me," she said, tripping over a leg of a bar stool and catching herself, "it's worth every fucking penny."

Chapter 20

Saturday, May 7.

In the morning, MacNeil woke to the sound of a waterfall of rain on the roof. He got up, padded around naked, made the coffee and did some preliminary stretches. Nobody could see into his windows unless they lived in the house across the street and had binoculars attached to their skull. He enjoyed the newness of his pad, the privacy, the "Adam" in his own Eden. A few of his one-night stands in Bucks County, enjoying his free spirit, said, "Wow, Woodstock is not dead."

The stretches revived him, then some primary calisthenics and pushups; the coffee was potent and he ate, showered, shaved. His beard had always been heavy and sometimes he had to shave twice if he had a function to go to in the evening. In the mirror he made a check list of his body, the hairy stomach still taut, the pecs and biceps starting to deflate and he made a note to double the morning workout since the nearest gym he knew of was in Atlantic City. He admired his chest hair and the trunk of his legs and his groin and smiled when he recalled one person describing him as "a nice guy to talk to, but truly a beast in the bedroom."

Christ, he was vain.

He was 32, single, sexual, like anyone else, but made a point to be discreet when he wanted to get laid. "Don't fuck where you live," a co-worker once told him. "Drive up to the city or fly to Chicago if you want to do stuff without the whole fucking town knowing about it." Odd coming from him since he was married but clearly knew the ropes.

MacNeil always wondered if he would be happier in a large city like Philadelphia or New York. Nah, he told himself, he couldn't cut the rat race. Those detectives worked their balls off and ended up, for the most part, the ones he *knew* anyway, bitter, depressed, and usually alcoholic.

His father was still alive, still a drunk, still living in his hometown of Biddeford, Maine, and so far, still held a job, played poker, went bowling, played golf and somehow drove home, in winter or in summer without killing someone or getting busted. He told his dad once, "Don't come crying to me from a jail and expect your badass detective son to rescue your sorry butt!"

"I wouldn't trust your fucking fairy ass to do anything!"

That was a memorable Christmas.

He shook his head of that screaming match and dressed. He wore the jacket he had last night, found his umbrella under the bed and walked over to the station.

Cape May had its own newspaper, and MacNeil made a habit of never reading any press when he was on a case. He learned that secret in Buck's County because the sensationalism of their news tended to overload, or rather, embellish the facts. Facts were boring, facts were simple and often, didn't interest readers. A dead body in the canal became a bloated, unrecognizable corpse in a leaf infested, green algae-d pool of stagnant water.

As Ginsberg once said, "Kill the little darlings."

He carried that habit here. The local paper was lying on his desk, there was one on everyone's desk and he didn't open it, but dropped it off at the front area for someone else to read. He left the rest of the gym membership names in Kurtz's message box for him to investigate with a note explaining he wanted this done by 1 PM in time for their briefing with Sgt. Ricca.

Gwen and John Parker were already there and MacNeil glanced at the clock. They were ten minutes early. They looked calm and rested, like they were waiting for a flight, and he was expecting fidgeting and a 'when are you going to reopen the gym?' anticipation on their faces.

"Good morning, Mr. and Mrs. Parker, thank you for coming." He inwardly winced when he saw Gwen Parker's face that read, 'What is this, a cocktail party?'

They stood up and MacNeil put up a hand. "I want to talk to you separately. Mrs. Parker, would you follow me, Mr. Parker, you can stay here." No room for debate or an argument. Gwen did a double take to her husband but followed MacNeil to his office. He sat down, but she stood in the doorway looking at the room like it was a coach's office in some smelly old high school and her frown intensified when she saw the trash can hadn't been emptied, the now two-day old coffee cups were sitting in there as if to confirm that yes, this place is pretty slipshod, like our investigating.

MacNeil was about to apologize for the look of the room when he stopped. *To hell with it.*

"Have a seat, please." She saw the two brown chairs and sat in one, her back straight waiting for the lice.

"Mrs. Parker. Can you tell me again who has keys to the gym?"

"Like I told you, Detective," she got huffy and then it dawned on her, MacNeil saw, that the routine questions had a purpose, looking for discrepancies, looking for lies, and she lost her attitude of superiority. "John, Wendell, Alex, and I have keys."

"Did you have any duplicates?"

"Yes, there is one duplicate. We have it at home."

"And you are sure that it is there?"

Gwen seemed surprised. "Well, of course it's there. It hangs on a tiny hook just past the front door. John and I agreed it would stay there in case there ever were an emergency."

"And has there ever been an 'emergency' where you had to use it?"

"No, Detective, we're both very reliable when it comes to the not losing the key to the gym. I leave mine on my car ring. John does the same."

"Mrs. Parker, have you ever slept with Alex Kearney?"

Her face registered nothing. She opened her purse and pulled out a cigarette and a lighter. She started to light when MacNeil said, "There's no smoking in my office, Mrs. Parker."

Not a ruffle. Not an apology or a smirk. She looked down at the trash can full of cigarette butts, said nothing, reloaded the cigarette in its package and dumped it and the lighter in her purse.

"Detective, what if I said, 'yes'?"

"Well-"

"What if I said, 'no'? Would it make a difference? Are you going to ask the same question to John? Probably not. What galls me is this presumption."

"It's not a presumption, Mrs. Parker, it's a question, yes or no."

"It's a presumption, Mr. MacNeil. John and I started the gym twelve years ago. It took a lot of work, work which I wasn't afraid of: rewiring, machine breakage, a couple of minor floods, backed up toilets, I've seen it all. I've also seen a lot of men waltz in there like they were god's gift to women, strutting, posing in the mirrors. I didn't care, Detective, I really didn't. I still don't. Men act very differently when they're around each other than when women are on the scene. Except for me. Initially, I worked-"

"I know, Mrs. Parker, most of the day."

"Let me finish. Yes, most of the day. Cleaning up after people, wiping the sweat, taking their money, making small talk, I wanted the gym to succeed. There were also the cat calls, the whistles, the looks that stripped me of every ounce of clothing. The entitlement, Detective. The entitlement to say whatever they felt like saying: 'Hey, baby cakes, sit on my face and let me bench press that!' 'You think my bicep's huge, sweet-heart, check out my dick.' They grabbed their crotches, the hard-ons in their shorts that they displayed right in front of me. They knew they couldn't whip it out, but they left nothing to the imagination.

"It's the presumption, Detective, it's the feeling that they could say whatever they wanted, and they got away with it. Well, not all of them. Some I kicked out. I warned them about their attitude, and they thought I was kidding. One got pissed off and threw a rock through a window, but the cops were able to find him. He wasn't very bright because he threw the rock in the middle of the day.

"John understood. He agreed when I said I would open, but stay only until 10 AM and take a back seat, focusing on money and bills and upkeep. It's been pretty decent. John says the clients don't get that raunchy without someone to direct their words to, and I frankly don't give a shit what they do or not do.

"But for you to ask me a question like that about Alex, why not go all out, Detective? Why not ask me if I sleep with all the clients? Why not ask me if I make it a regular habit to seduce the college boys or hump a new customer or bang the old guy who feels 30 again, god almighty, Detective, where does it stop?

"Just because I'm the woman in this sad drama, you automatically pin all these sexual misdoings on me. Alex was a good man. I liked him. He was cocky at times, yes, I told you that. Yes, he was kind and sweet natured and good with the clients. So, to answer your question, Detective, my response to you is this unequivocable, unashamed answer," she paused for breath. "Guess!"

MacNeil absorbed it all. The Gwen Parker monologue wasn't rehearsed, it wasn't an affect. He saw how she made a life for herself, with John, without John, knowing what she wanted, knowing that Cape May could potentially slide into yet another beach town with a giant boardwalk and rides and the smell of fried dough forever in the air. She fought for its integrity just as she fought for the integrity of the gym.

"Thank you, Mrs. Parker," he admitted, "that harassment is unforgiveable." He let down his guard, maybe a mistake, "When this murder is solved, and the gym is back on its feet, if you ever experience that again, call the police."

Gwen registered nothing. She was used to registering nothing when it came to men promising, or pleading, or the standard, 'I'll pay you next week, Gwen, when the check clears.' "Is there anything else?"

MacNeil turned back to his notes. He scanned the first page, pretending to look for something pertinent. "Did you sit in on Alex's interview when he first applied?"

"Yes, I did."

"How did it go?"

"What do you mean?"

"Was Alex nervous, uptight, desperate even to get the job?"

"Detective, I don't think I've ever seen Alex Kearney nervous or uptight or desperate in the short months I've known him. He was twenty-four years old, and seemed to not have a care in the world. The interview was pretty straight forward, we asked him questions, he answered them, John gave him some scenarios-"

"What do you mean, 'scenarios'?"

"He would say to Alex, 'What would you do if someone was overweight but wanted to get stronger?' or 'When someone is bench pressing and their feet are like this' – John would get on a bench to demonstrate – 'what's wrong with this technique?' Things like that."

"And Alex knew his business?"

She smiled. "Oh, yeah, he knew so much about anatomy and physiology. He was bouncing out words like 'anaerobic' and 'aerobic' and linking vitamin intake to certain diets and frankly, I'm laughing a little because he wouldn't shut up."

"Do you think your husband is a jealous man?"

Her smiled dropped. "What's that supposed to mean?"

MacNeil shrugged. "I don't know, have you ever noticed him cringe or glare at another man who was checking you out, say, in a restaurant or at a concert?"

She shut down. "You'll have to ask him."

"Now, you two were home all night after John closed up the gym, the night Alex was killed."

"Yes."

"What did you do?"

"We talked. John took a shower. I had made a pot roast, potatoes, a salad, we talked some more," and she looked him dead in the eye, "and then we made love." Not an ounce of embarrassment.

"What time did you, um, finish?"

"I don't know, Detective, I'm not in the habit of checking the clock after I'm done fucking."

She was starting to turn. The battle had begun again. MacNeil was glad. If he could get her angry, something might spill out.

"What time do you usually get up in the morning when you have to work at the gym?" Curve balls. Curve balls.

"At 4:30 AM. I enjoy the silence."

"And John stays asleep?"

"Yes."

"You live on Pinetree Drive, in the Villas, is that correct?"

"You know it is, Detective."

"Alex lived on Oregon Ave. That's not far from your house at all. Have you ever had Alex over for dinner or a party?"

"No."

"Have you ever been to his apartment?"

"No. Never."

MacNeil made some notes. He closed the book and stood up. "When you arrived at the gym yesterday morning, did you notice Alex's car parked in the next block?"

"No, I didn't."

"Thank you, Mrs. Parker."

She stood up, reserved, if she was peeved, she didn't show it. "Detective MacNeil, when can we reopen the gym?"

"Monday, should be about right. I will confirm that with you and John."

"Monday, May 9th?"

"Yes, but it's a tentative 'yes'. If I have to change that, I'll let you know."

He followed Gwen back to the main lobby, she knew her way around the place. John stood up with a 'so, what happened?' face and she kissed him on the lips. "Your turn, dear." She had no intention of soothing or placating or arguing or debating anything.

John, for some reason, wore a tie, and a clean pair of corduroys. He too had a look of disdain in MacNeil's office, the smell of cigarette butts, the coffee. MacNeil hauled up the ugly trash can and put it outside. God, he thought, this place looks like a two-bit garage or a slimy restaurant, how do we expect people to take us seriously when the place is a dump. He'd talk to the Chief when this interview was over.

"Have a seat, Mr. Parker," MacNeil pointed and sat behind his desk. He didn't really want to use the desk as a power front, but if he sat on the desk, he'd be a good three feet higher than Parker and that kind of psychological intimidation never worked. He opened his notebook.

"I wanted to ask you some questions about the gym. First of all, you came in at 10 every day and worked until 8 PM, is that correct?"

"Yes, every week day. On the weekends, I opened the place at 6 and stayed all day."

"That's a lot of hours, sir, if you don't know that already."

"It is. But Alex worked Saturdays and Sundays, so many times, when he didn't have a client, he'd work the front desk and I could leave, or do an errand, get lunch, that sort of thing. It wasn't much and he was happy to do it. Half the time when I returned, he was pitching his training, getting new clients."

"But during the week day, you couldn't leave."

"Yes, that's right. I usually brought a lunch, I had a thermos with coffee in it usually, and ate dinner when I got home."

"The back door to the gym is always locked. You know that's a fire violation. Why did you do that?"

John Parker hit every ball like he knew every trick in the pitcher's sleeve. "Yeah, I know, and if you have to fine me, fine me. When I kept it unlocked, the gym guys would sneak their friends in. I couldn't watch the whole place, and they

123

knew it too. For the first few years, it was open, and if I was on the phone or talking to someone in the office, they waited until they saw their chance. It was like they had a code or something. They'd pop open the door a crack, the other guy would crawl in, go into the locker room, change and come out like everyone else. God, that would piss me off!"

"So how did you find out?"

"Detective, some people just aren't very bright. It's like the dumb kids in school who'd sneak in late through a window or forge their parent's signature on a report card. Those clowns thought they were invisible or something, but they always got caught and had that surprised dopey look sitting in the principal's office waiting for their sentence." He sighed. "Some guys don't grow up. It was obvious. After being here a few years, I started to know everyone who was a member, head count, or by looks, or ages, I don't know, it's like raising chickens. When suddenly this new face is lying on his back, lifting weights trying to disappear into the bench, the guilt made it clear. So, I got their names, kicked them out, threatened to call the cops if they gave me any lip, and told them never to come in here again. And, I locked the only other door into the place."

"And if there were a fire?"

John Parker shuffled in his chair. "I'd break the windows in the locker room. Everyone could stand on a bench and crawl out. Look, Detective, if you've got a better idea, let me know."

"Was there any window broken recently, in the past week or so?"

"No."

"Alex didn't live far from you over in the Villas, did you know that?"

"Yes, I did."

"Did you two ever get together in his apartment, or meet at a bar, have a drink?"

"No, Detective, I'm an alcoholic, so sitting in a bar is not something I do."

"Excuse me, sir. Forgive my insensitivity. Did he ever ask to talk to you outside of work?"

"Not that I remember. We talked enough at the gym."

"Did he ever confide in you, Mr. Parker?"

"Confide?" A look out the window and a half smirk. "'Bout what?"

"Well, he's young, he's alone in this town. Sometimes a man will talk to another man, someone who's older, someone he respects, ask for advice about, I don't know, anything, buying a car, taking a class, saving money, dating, women, any one of those things."

John swept the ceiling trying to remember anything, or doing a good job of *pretending* to remember something. "Nothin' that seemed important. Sometimes he'd tell a story about the Coast Guard, or a drinking binge he had up in Alaska. He'd talk about his dad, he liked his dad and told me he tried to make sure he called him once a week." John

Parker seemed a bit touched at that show of affection. "You know, Detective, I only knew Alex for about eight months. He didn't confide in me on anything serious, I think he had his dad for that. He was a young guy, I figured he had his own friends, or making new ones."

"Did he ever work out when the gym was open?"

"He used to, back when he first started, but it got too annoying for him. Word got around that he was the newly hired trainer, and these men had no qualms about interrupting his routine, asking him questions about training, or asking him what weight they should use knowing full well if they could get some free advice and not have to hire him for a private session, they would. He got sick of it. That's when he asked me if he could work out after hours."

"Did he ever come by with a girlfriend?"

John chuckled. "Oh, I don't know if I'd call them girlfriends. Sometimes, a girl would be waiting for him outside at the end of his shift, or a girl would call asking if he was working that day; sometimes a girl dropped him off. Sometimes I'd see him around town talking to the ladies, he had a great smile, Detective, and he knew how to use it."

"Did you ever see him hanging around with men his age?"

"No, I haven't. Maybe somebody else has. He had so much interaction with men here, maybe he wanted to be around the women for the other half of the day. He was young, Detective, he was looking to get laid, isn't that all any of us wanted at that age?"

"Are you a jealous man, Mr. Parker?"

John Parker didn't see that slippery ball. He hesitated, as if he couldn't remember what day it was. "No, I don't think any more than anyone else. What would I be jealous of?"

"Alex."

"Alex?"

"He's young, like you said, he gets laid, he's strong, built, attractive, maybe you started to think Gwen might want to-"

"If I could tell you to fuck yourself, Detective, without being thrown in the slammer, I would."

"Lots of men feel jealous, it's part of-"

"Alex Kearney was not the only man in the gym with a good body, a lot of charm and in his mid-twenties, Detective. If I were jealous of every cocky fucker that walked into the place, I would throw it all in and drive a cab."

"Mr. Parker, did you kill Alex Kearney?"

"Because I was jealous of him?!"

"Because of any reason."

"No, Detective. I did not."

"Did Alex ever not show up on a Saturday?"

"I'm getting a little tired of the cat and mouse, Detective, if you want to know something, say it."

"Okay, did Alex ever not show up on a Saturday? No hidden agenda."

"Yeah, sometimes he did. He always asked me well in advance for the day off, and he rearranged the clients' sessions with them himself."

"Do you know why he wanted Saturday off?"

"Not really. He said he liked to go to Atlantic City sometimes, and Saturdays was what he preferred."

"Did he ever say what he did up there?"

"No, and I never asked." John shrugged. "My guess is he liked to gamble."

"Do you think he had a problem? Maybe he got over his head in debt?"

"If he did, he never told me. He never asked me for money or a loan. If he had problems paying his rent, ask his landlord. Are we through?"

"Almost. On the night Alex was killed, you were home, is that right?"

"Yes, and I never left."

"Did Gwen leave?"

"No."

MacNeil knew the two of them had their story all intact, all thought out. He went on anyway. "So, what did you do that night?"

"I came home. Took a shower. Gwen made some dinner and after that we got together, curled up, relaxed."

That's a euphemism I never heard before.

"Mr. Parker, as I said to your wife, the gym, in my estimation, will be ready to reopen next Monday, May 9th. I trust that is good news."

"Are we through?"

"Yes, thank you." He stood up.

"I know my way out of here, Detective." In the hall he tripped over the trash can, and papers, cigarette butts, and two cups of dried disgusting coffee spilled on the wooden floor and scattered across the hall. Needless to say, John Parker never stopped.

At that moment, the front desk sergeant popped his head in while avoiding the coffee stains. "Sir, Sean Kearney, Alex's father, is here. He drove down to identify the body and the Coroner told him you'd like to see him."

Chapter 21

The sergeant returned with Mr. Kearney who didn't walk, but slumped into MacNeil's office, his wet jacket splashed against the door, his body twisted in pain as he cried and he held onto the walls and the chair like he was about to pass out. MacNeil whispered, "Sergeant, I know it's not your job, but would you get the broom and a pan and sweep up this mess?" as he pointed to the debris in the hallway that Mr. Kearney just sloshed his feet through.

"Yes, sir."

"Sergeant, would you first get Mr. Kearney a glass of water, please," the detective took the man's arm and guided him into a chair. "Sir, sit a minute, don't talk." The sergeant left.

Sean Kearney was 52 years old, and outside of losing his wife when Alex was ten, he never had a shock as bad as this. His face was pale as a snowbank, his hands were shaking, and he continued to cry. MacNeil pulled over the other tawdry wooden chair and held his hand.

"Alex!" the man moaned, "Alex! My son!" He leaned over. "Oh, Christ, I'm going to be sick!"

MacNeil panicked for a second, thought fast, raced to the desk and pulled out the top drawer that he used for pencils and envelopes and scissors. He dumped the contents on his desk and placed the empty drawer in Mr. Kearney's lap as the man wretched up what looked like an omelet and chunks of toast.

MacNeil ran down to the men's room, yanked on a myriad of paper towels, wet them and raced back as the man was trying to wipe his mouth and figure out what to do with a wet wooden drawer. MacNeil placed the paper towels in the man's hand and used some to wipe the man's mouth. "Get a moment, sir, don't try to talk, it's okay."

The sergeant returned with the water, and as MacNeil exchanged that for the drawer, with a look that read, 'Don't say a damn thing, get rid of this.'

MacNeil shut his office door and returned to the wooden chair. He reached for the man's hand again. They sat in silence as Alex's father, in his cheap pants and checkered shirt kept his head between his legs and rocked until the nausea left him. Five minutes went by of nothing but silence and sobs. MacNeil thought of his own father and how this tableau would never be in his family movie. His heart broke for Mr. Kearney, the worst part of this job, witnessing the torment, the anguish, the disbelief of death, and the harsh, cold reality that he was outliving his own son's life.

MacNeil took two wet towels and washed the back of the man's neck, rubbed his forehead and then his hands. The man looked up with a grateful surprise and the color in his face returned. He drank some water. "Thank you, Detective."

MacNeil almost hugged the man, his arms were reaching out, but he thought that might be too much affection, not because they were men, but because he wanted to maintain his professionalism.

To hell with professionalism.

He pulled his chair closer and draped an arm around the man's wet shoulders and the man sighed in relief. It was as if he were waiting for someone to show him some kindness after the hell he went through. The shock of an early morning phone call yesterday from the Cape May Police had him stammering on the phone to his boss at the paper mill, stumbling into the car and driving the eight hours or so, he lost count, to arrive at the bottom of New Jersey.

"Mr. Kearney, I'm sorry for the death of your son. Truly sorry."

Sean Kearney teared up all over again, but kept his composure. He leaned his arms across his legs and looked up at the detective with blank blue eyes. MacNeil felt a sadness in his throat and sat quietly until it passed.

"Mr. Kearney, John Parker, the man who owns the gym, said that you and Alex were very close."

"He was our only child."

"He called you every month, yes?"

133

"Every two weeks." Mr. Kearney seemed grateful for the calming facts, the information. "Sometimes once a week."

"He called simply to see how you were doing, yes?"

"Yeah, I guess. We had a good bond, we always had, sometimes he called and talked about, I don't know, stupid stuff, this town, a girl he was seeing, feeling like he was becoming his own man."

"That's a good memory. That's what dads and sons do when they have a good relationship."

"We had that."

"Did he ever mention a girl by name?"

Mr. Kearney chuckled. "God, he was always going on about some girl he met, he's been that way since high school. Frankly, Detective, I stopped listening, it felt like they were just another notch on his bedpost." He stopped and turned to the man. "I don't think any of them were serious.

"Sometimes he talked how he helped out with the Boy Scouts or asked my advice when he fixed people's wiring when there was a problem in their homes. He had joined this group called "Christ's Carpenters" connected to one of the churches here, I don't know which one. He had a big heart, he did it all for free."

"Mr. Kearney, did Alex ever tell you about anything that was bothering him such as a debt, or someone who was harassing him, maybe even a jealous boyfriend or husband he accidentally set off?" He saw Alex's father about to talk. "Please, sir, take a minute and think and try to remember."

The man looked at the window opposite, above MacNeil's desk and watched the rain pour against the panes like a hose. It was the only noise in the room, the constant slamming of the water and it reminded MacNeil of the shower where he found Alex.

"No, sir. Nothing comes to mind."

"Alex had a job at a gym in Oswego. From what I gather, he drove to work every day, lived with you at your home, the home he grew up in. Sounds like a perfect set up: good job, no rent, so why did Alex leave Scriba?"

"Detective, Alex was a simple man. He joined the Coast Guard, saw a bit of the world, mostly Alaska, found some interests and did them. He wasn't the college type; he never would be. He didn't want to be. He was a small-town boy, Detective, he liked the country, liked the small-town lifestyle, liked to fish, hang out with his friends. He didn't want to go to a big city, not even Rochester, he wasn't made for that. I think he moved away because he wanted to see what he could do on his own, don't we all do that? I can't say I blamed him. He was young, liked the ladies, had his own place, what's better than that?"

"So, there was no shotgun wedding that he slunk out of town over?"

The man smiled. "Nah, Detective, Alex wasn't always bright, but he wasn't dumb either. Scriba's too small of a town not to have heard of that."

135

MacNeil didn't have the heart, the integrity, the what, he couldn't find the word, maybe it was the courage, to tell this man that his son shot porn. Maybe it was simply that the information would do nothing to further the case and it would only upset the man even more than he already was. He turned the channel. "Where are you staying right now, sir?"

Mr. Kearney seemed sad that the conversation had moved away from Alex. "Um, it's at this place called the, uh," he had to think, "the Driftwood Motor Lodge," he concluded. "I want to go to Alex's apartment."

"Of course. I have Alex's car keys and we can ride over in his car if you like. I'll drive. You can stay there tonight if you wish or take whatever keepsakes you want. I did, however, take the photograph of you and Alex, do you know the one I mean?"

A soft sigh of recognition. "Yes."

"I have that one with me to show people when I interview them. A lot of people didn't know who Alex was, but the photograph jars their memory."

"Of course."

"I will keep it safe. I will give it back to you, when-" *when what? Alex's murderer was found.*

"That's fine."

"If you don't want to spend the night in his apartment, Mr. Kearney, I understand. I can take you back to the Driftwood. Stay there another night, sir, if you wish and you can go home tomorrow. Don't worry about the cost, I'll call them up and have the town pay for it. You might think of something between now and then and if you do, please call me." He pulled out yet another of his cards and placed it in Sean Kearney's palm. "If you feel like eating again, go to the C-View, it's not expensive and it's probably a place Alex would have gone to, it has good food." He dug into his wallet and pulled out a twenty. "Take it, for food, for gas, for whatever you need." The man resisted, but MacNeil placed that firmly in his palm as well. "We can release Alex today and he will be transported back to Scriba to any funeral home you decide."

"Monahan's," the older man said barely a whisper. "It's the only one in town."

"Monahan's. Fine. That's fine. I will tell the Coroner." MacNeil helped the man to his feet and opened the door. "Thank you for answering some questions, today."

Mr. Kearney wasn't listening. "He'll be with his mother, now," he said.

Chapter 22

C hris MacNeil called the landlord to let him know they were coming. He drove the man to Alex's apartment, and the moment he pulled into the tiny driveway, Ted Small appeared, umbrella open, moving to the car. He carried an extra apartment key with him and he went to the passenger side and opened the door.

"Mr. Kearney, I'm Ted Small, Alex's landlord," he waited as Sean Kearney got out of the car and when under the shelter of the umbrella, he proceeded to give him a strong hug. "I liked Alex a lot, he was a good man. I'm sorry for your loss."

"Thank you." Mr. Kearney looked as if he were about to start crying again, and Ted Small put his arm around him. "This is the key to his apartment," he nodded over to the yellow painted walls above the garage. "Mr. Kearney, I want to honor your privacy, so if you want to go up there alone, you can. I have nothing planned for my day today, so if you want me to go with you, I will. You can tell me all about your boy. You're welcome to stay up there tonight, or stay here in the house, sometimes it's good to talk and I'm here to listen. I have some wonderful memories about Alex and if you want the company, I'm here."

Sean Kearney was clearly moved by the offer and this time, he was hesitant. He looked at MacNeil and the car and then back at the apartment and then at MacNeil.

"I can call a patrol car to pick me up, sir," MacNeil explained. "I'll go to the Driftwood and pay the bill and bring your clothes over here if you want. Don't worry about a thing."

Kearney looked at Ted Small and he saw the kinship, the common goodness in the landlord's face and he sighed as if a stranger had stopped to rescue him and his stranded vehicle in the middle of the night.

"Yes," he said, "I want to do that. Thank you." MacNeil gave him Alex's car keys. "Oh, here," Sean Kearney dug into his pockets, "the keys to my car if someone could drive that over. It's a 1970 blue Ford Impala."

"Of course."

"The phone's inside Detective, help yourself," Ted Small whispered and led Mr. Kearney up the stairs, like a ministering angel guiding a lost soul home. "Tell me about Alex," he said, "and where did you meet his mother?"

Their conversation was intimate, quiet, slowly disappearing into the air as the two men ascended the stairs. The rain had stopped, suddenly, like a turn in a person's life, a moment of darkness into a moment of sunshine. MacNeil ducked into Ted Small's house, made the calls, and waited at the end of the driveway for the patrol car. He checked out Mr. Kearney from the Driftwood, packed the clothes and toiletries into Kearney's tiny, brown suitcase, found the Impala and gave the keys to the patrol officer's partner to drive it back to Oregon Avenue. He didn't want a lift to his office. He preferred to walk.

Ideas and theories swirled in his head. Three people had opportunity: Gwen or John Parker and Wendell Taylor, the maintenance man. A very, ridiculously easy opportunity for any of them to sneak in, kill Alex, and sneak out, lock the door. Everything would be above board, no raised eyebrow from a snoopy neighbor.

Why? Why would anyone kill Alex Kearney? He was well-liked, friendly, cocky, a little vain, flirtatious, but those are ridiculous reasons unless he was dealing with a psychotic personality.

Alex could have let someone in after John and Taylor went home. That's easy to do, but why? And why would the killer bother to lock the door behind him using Alex's key? If your point is to kill the man and get it done quickly, why take the time to ensure normalcy?

MacNeil's inner guidance was on automatic pilot. He walked down streets without thinking where they took him. He started on Beach Ave, past the shops and construction and the newly renovated areas designed to bring in more tourists. The breeze was oddly perfect for early May.

Gwen Parker did have a point. Without some kind of brakes on development, this whole town could turn into one cloud of cotton candy and fried dough. He turned left on Jackson Street and admired the Victorians. The Mad Batter had only been open for a year, and he could predict it, with the bar and the outdoor dining, to be a big hit this summer.

The walking gave him room to think and sometimes he talked out loud, usually when a person was walking past, giving him the once over either due to his handsome frame or his saying, "Who the hell *killed* him?"

The Washington Mall came up on his left and he headed away from the people strolling there, not many at this time of year, but the feel of Cape May's charm hummed, and people, whether they knew it or not, hummed with it.

He popped into Della's again and the same girl who worked before was there. He ordered a hamburger and coffee and took out his notebook. His badge flipped out and he saw her staring at it when she brought over the coffee.

"You a cop?"

"I'm a detective, I work for the county."

"So, you're working on that Alex Kearney murder?"

MacNeil winced. He hated the theatrics some people used, like they were auditioning for a bad movie.

"Yes, I am. I've been assigned to that case."

The woman put down her coffee pot and bit her lip, looking around hoping no one saw her. "I was going to stop at the police station after my shift. Alex was my boyfriend and

I'm scared. I don't want what happened to him to happen to me."

MacNeil was stumped. "Your boyfriend!" *What took you so long?*

"Yeah, we've been together a little more than a month. I don't want to die, man!"

"I understand, what's your name?"

"Abigail Starbird."

"I'm Detective MacNeil. What time do you get off work here?"

"2:00."

"When you're done, come down to the station and ask for me." He pulled out his card. "You're not in trouble, I want to talk to you about Alex, and obviously, this is not the time."

"Miss!" A voice from her far left.

"Okay," she whispered, "2:00. Thank you."

Chapter 23

*W*hat took us so long, Kip? I think we both wanted something that could be sustainable, how's that for a 21st century buzzword? Sustainable. We dove in, cautiously, and I could see your constant fear of the future, two steps forward, one step back. Anita Bryant wouldn't happen until October, and you and I had a good laugh over that. That was the same summer, where in August, they closed the Cape May beaches for six days due to sewage overload. I think you had something to do with that. Not the sewage overload, but the waving the warning flags to the EPA. If the beach is closed, it's the same thing as the town being closed.

You and I used that time and drove to Ogunquit and stayed in Montgomery Clift's old hangout. You felt very debonair. Didn't you grow a beard? You said you wanted to fit in with the locals. I said, I don't think sitting on the porch and drinking a $20 Sauvignon Blanc was exactly 'fitting in'.

Marriage wasn't an option. Living together would have raised eyebrows, but in some ways, who would have cared? It might have been the straw that broke the camel's back.

So much has changed. Today, Alex's murder would have been solved in probably five hours, we have plastic yellow CRIME SCENE tape to reduce contamination, DNA testing, and infrared cameras that can detect so many clues, wrap up so many mysteries.

Love, however, gratefully, still takes a lifetime.

Chapter 24

MacNeil paid the bill, wrapped the rest of his burger in a napkin and walked back to the office. Ricca and Kurtz were there, filling him in on nothing. They had interviewed and re-interviewed everyone on the list, alone, in private, away from a boss, or a wife or any other distraction.

For Sgt. Peter Ricca, many of these men were people he knew from high school; he wormed his way in through the small-town connection: the older brother of his classmate, the baseball star in the Senior class, the 3rd youngest in a family of boys. They all, whether they wanted to or not, had the connections, the cousin who married his sister, the daughter who was Prom Queen, the matrix was astonishing if anyone ever wanted to draw it and he was one part of this giant web. His small frame was laughable for a cop, but most of the men didn't see that. They talked freely, but Ricca knew when they were masking something and often, it was the common basic fact that some of these men were embarrassed. Embarrassed at getting older, losing their shape, losing their hair, losing their sex appeal, therefore, turning, with a vulnerable nod, a shy appeal, to Alex, younger, stronger, more fit, cockier, energetic, who, for a fee, would pump back into them the sexual longing they may have lost, which, through their delusional bond with the younger man, in their working out, they created the misguided unrealistic notion that they never lost it in the first place.

Ricca noticed and calculated all of it and as an insider, gave them permission, it seemed, to be that exposed. It was either that, or arrest them for murder.

For Kurtz, the rookie, many of the men looked down on him, patronized him, two even laughed at him when he knocked on their door. But his approach wasn't like his co-worker. He had a brilliant memory despite his rudimentary demeanor and his biceps and legs which, instead of making him seem more in authority, made him look like an extra in a cop movie. When he showed up at their door with no notebook or pen, just himself, hand on hips, chest pushing against his shirt, trying to look tough, a strange metamorphosis took over. The men he interviewed scoffed or smirked at first, then Kurtz, simply by never writing in a notebook, was able to maintain a strong, unflinching eye contact. It was a mental battle in many regards. For some of the men, the eyes became intimidating, not because Kurtz was older, he wasn't, or had a lot of power, he didn't, but because his eyes bore into the men's soul. For many, it reminded them of teachers, or nuns or priests who determinedly demanded where the missing homework was or why he failed a Latin test, because eventually, each in his own way, realized the balance of power was not through strength or age or position or wealth, but through the intensity of Kurtz's eyes behind the questions.

"Jesus, nothing?!" MacNeil was incredulous. He barely knew these two men, and interrogating suspects was tough work, it was easy to become complacent and give up after one or two questions. But he trusted these men. He had to and he had to honor the fact that they were townies, they knew this area inside and out and they knew the typical male behavior - from the fishermen to the barflies – and who in that masculine circle was considered 'trouble', who was trying to shed a bad reputation, and who was keeping his nose clean.

The two cops had written up their reports and MacNeil glanced through them quickly, scanning for a circled word, or something underlined in red, or an asterisk. Nothing.

"Gentlemen, think, think. Alex Kearney was young, horny, good looking, and got laid. Now, you'd think there'd be a jealous husband, or a pissed-off father or *some motive*, that would cause one of these men to go into that locker room and pulverize that man's balls! It doesn't take Freud to know that those fuckers were what got Alex killed."

The two men sitting opposite him nodded. They agreed. They had scoured the lists; they knew the family connections. Silence.

MacNeil undid the string on the confidential Coroner's report that was on his desk when he returned. He read it to the two men.

"Alex Kearney. Caucasian Male. 24 years old. 5'10", 185 lbs. Cause of Death was severe hemorrhaging due to traumatic brain injury in the skull. Hit several times by a heavy object. No drugs or poisons found in his body. No damage to the liver. Lungs, heart, healthy. Testicles crushed after death by a heavy object."

In an ironic, morbid, completely unprofessional way, all three men sighed at the same time, and Ricca said it out loud, "Christ, I'm glad he didn't have to feel that while he was alive."

MacNeil had asked the men not to interview the Boy Scout Leader, Ray Dieter. He called Dieter now and asked if he could speak with him at his home. He would go there at 5 PM.

"Do either of you know Abigail Starbird?" the detective asked. "Blond hair, about 5'4", looks about twenty-two, works at Della's?"

Blank faces on both.

"She's not local?" MacNeil asked thinking, *I thought you all knew each other?*

"Don't know her, sir," said Sgt Ricca. "She's not local in that sense."

"Della's?" Kurtz snorted. "Sorry, sir, but I never go in there. I'm a C-View man myself."

MacNeil felt the jab, and almost smirked at his revelation. *That little shit.*

"She told me she had been dating Alex when he was killed. She's coming down to the station to talk to me. Did you two ever hear about her? Did any of the men mention her as a regular girlfriend?"

"No, sir." Kurtz added. "To be honest sir, most of these men didn't know Alex existed, I'd say about 75% of them worked out when Alex wasn't around. They knew the gym had a trainer, but they didn't seem to care or know who he was."

"So they *said*," MacNeil got huffy.

Kurtz put up his hand. "Yes, so they *said*. But, with all due respect, I know when a man is lying or evading something. It's instinctive in us. With a woman, I'll admit, she could probably lie through her teeth and I'd be drawn in hook, line, and sinker, but with men, there's something we have in common. I don't know what to call it, but when a man is giving you a line, even if you don't know the truth, you can call him on his bullshit very easily."

MacNeil shook his head, "Yeah, I understand. You've got the smarts, Kurtz, I hand that to you. Nobody can teach you that."

Ricca looked a wounded puppy waiting for his treat. MacNeil felt it more than saw it and was about to create some compliment for him too. *Fuck it, this isn't a kindergarten.*

He turned to the puppy. "Tell me about Matt Ryan, the bookstore owner. He said he was talking on the phone to his sister the night Alex was killed. Did that hold up?"

Sgt Ricca looked through his papers, acting almost like this was a more important suspect than the others when MacNeil wanted a simple 'yes' or 'no'. He let Ricca have his bit.

"He checks out, sir. I called the sister to verify-"

"You can't use a family mem-"

"-to *verify* the call. She did *and* Ryan's phone records show that that number was placed from his phone. Now if he got someone else to fill in while he smashed Kearney's skull, that would be a fucking first. Sir."

MacNeil admired the balls. "Thank you, Sgt. I'll put that in my notes. Thank you, gentlemen, for doing this legwork. It saves me a lot of time." They got up to go. "Hold it, one more thing." They sat down.

He pulled out the middle left side drawer for the large plastic folder of Alex's pornography magazines. He tossed out the gloves and when he brought the folder to his desktop, Kurtz's mouth dropped open.

"Keep it in your pants, Kurtz. I want scrutiny, not junior high school comments."

He removed the magazines, their paper quality extremely shoddy, and MacNeil laid them out so that they were upside down to him and right side up to his staff. "Did you ever hear of these magazines?"

"Yep." Kurtz said. "They're not "Penthouse", I can tell you that, sir." He unconsciously adjusted his crotch as he opened the first one. "They're pretty second-rate."

Ricca was taking a higher road. "You can see, sir, the quality of light was crap, high, intense, look at the shadows. They're not going for style here, sir, just full-on titillation."

MacNeil opened to the eight stills of the movie scene from "While my Husband is Away" with Alex. He pointed to the photo, misjudged the distance and his finger landed on Alex's butt. "This is Alex."

Despite his bravura and doing his best to avoid the women photos and suppress a hard-on, even Kurtz was impressed. "Christ, he was big boy, sir. He must have gotten a lot with that."

"Sort of irrelevant now, Kurtz. That's why I'm looking for a man who might have wanted Alex killed: banging his wife, girlfriend, his daughter, whatever. I can't imagine his murder being, sadly," MacNeil stopped for a moment at the pathetic rationing of human nature, "any more than that."

He opened the other magazines, showed them the scenes with Alex, and winced at the titles of the movies: "Blue Collar Baller", "Greased and Pumped", and "The Postman Always Cums Twice". "You two ever hear or see these, uh, films?"

Both men shook their head, no.

"Gentlemen, I'm not here to comment, I don't give a shit what you do in some skanky theater, just level with me, have you ever seen these before? Have you ever seen another movie with Alex in it?"

Kurtz was starting to drool over the women, but he pulled himself up, "If I did, I wouldn't remember the titles." He crossed his heart. "Scout's honor, sir." Ricca turned red and said nothing.

"How many porn theaters, the big ones, are there in Atlantic City?"

"I don't know exactly, sir," Kurtz started to look in the sky, counting. "They're off the Boardwalk. You're not talking about the peep shows?"

"No, the big theaters where they show XXX all day. Alex sometimes went up to AC, John Parker told me, but didn't tell me why." He pointed to the pictures again, "I think we can guess why. If there's a movie house that shows this, they might be connected to a movie, and I use this word loosely, 'studio'."

"Do me a favor, Sgt," he motioned to Ricca. "Get me a list of the porn theaters in AC, their addresses and phone numbers. Oh, while you're at it, include any strip clubs nearby. See if you can find the name of any movie producers or talent agents that obviously are into porn."

Ricca looked proud at the responsibility.

MacNeil filled out a request permission form asking the Chief for the ability to confiscate one of Alex's porn films. He listed their names and imagined the smirk in which the request would be received. He wrote that he didn't care which one they 'borrowed', and he almost heard the howls of laughter coming from down the hall.

The men left. MacNeil went to the bathroom, splashed cold water on his face, combed his hair, took a leak and was once again surprised at the reek of urine and the stains on the floor. He checked himself in the mirror and re-tucked his shirt, adjusted his pants so they were lined up off his hips. He re-tied the tie and gave a final onceover. He returned to his desk and typed a letter of formal request listing the unsightly, disgusting specific instances of neglect and uncleanliness in this station and demanding there'd be a regular clean-up crew hired for a weekly Friday night sanitation.

The window was open again, he didn't remember opening it, but the warm breeze drifted in blowing his notes around in a small whirlwind. He threw down books and a paperweight and contained everything. He put on gloves again, replaced Alex's magazines into the plastic folder and back in the drawer. He didn't think Abigail Starbird would have to be made aware of these. She seemed too innocent to be told that her boyfriend was a hired stud for pornography.

MacNeil typed up his notes, filed away his reports, had his notebook open. He walked to the main lounge behind the lobby. The smell of coffee hit him before he walked through the door. Someone had made a fresh brew and despite the horrible Styrofoam cups that made his teeth cringe and the Carnation Instant (*Get some damn milk in this place!*), he silently thanked whoever took the trouble to do this. He moved toward the back, checked for mail and messages in his mail box, found none, then straightened up his shoulders for another weeping scene.

Abigail Starbird hadn't changed clothes, she looked like a waitress in a cheap movie and MacNeil wondered if she ever had to wear that for a night of fantasy sex with Alex. He shook his head and slapped himself for the contradictory thoughts in his head. She looked up when she heard his footsteps, an anxious look, almost startled, like someone had the handcuffs ready because that's what happens to anybody who dares visit the police station. She carried a large shoulder bag that was covered in squares. Each square had a different design on it, blue lines on one, a peace sign on another, the "OM" symbol, red circles, green horizontal lines, every inch ablaze in color. The strap was wide and cotton looking and she clutched the bag like it was a baby. Her brown hair wasn't rolled up for work, now it was loose and hanging straight down her back. She looked like one of those girls in high school who couldn't sing very well and so was relegated to "Girl's Chorus", the lowest singing group for all the leftover people.

"Abigail?" The detective smiled. "Hi, thank you for coming. Again, my name is MacNeil, Chris MacNeil."

She said nothing. She stood up and waited, he guessed, for him to make the first move. "Let's go back to my office, there's privacy there."

She was mute. She followed him through the door, down the smelly, dusty hallway, and entered his office. She didn't seem to care if it was a polished movie set or a dumped over tumble of mismatched tables and chairs.

He motioned to a chair for her as he sat on the edge of his desk doing his best to look relaxed, and not like some hip history teacher who wanted to rap. Nothing helped. "Abigail, are you alright?"

"Yes," she said.

"Do you want something to drink? The coffee is fresh."

She winced, like being asked to work a double. "No, thank you."

He dove in. "So, first of all, I'm sorry about Alex. This must be hard for you."

She looked away for a second, almost as if the mention of his name would set her off. "Thank you."

MacNeil opened his notebook.

"I want to find the person who did this. That's all, that's my job. How old are you, Abigail?"

"I'm 20. Man, do you want to see my driver's license?" She started fidgeting in her pockets.

"When you find it. How long have you known Alex?"

She stopped searching.

Christ, is she going to keep freezing every time I ask a question? This is like interviewing a deer.

"I don't know, I'd say since the end of February." She found the paper and handed it over to him. "We met at the C-View."

The license read Abigail Starbird, September 1, 1956. Her address was registered at 661 Town Bank Rd.

"Do you live in an apartment?" he asked. He wasn't as swift about placing addresses as Ricca and Kurtz were.

"Kind of. It's a studio pad on the top floor of these people's house. They're cool. They renovated it, it's small, but it's nice up there. It gets lots of heat."

"You met Alex at the C-View, just by chance? Through a friend? A blind date?"

Abigail smiled. She was transported back to that night, he could tell. Her eyes got a tad misty.

Don't cry on me. Please, god, don't cry on me.

"Nothing like that. I was there with my friend Lori Beth and we were talking and having a beer and checking out the crowd. Alex walked in and sat alone at the bar. It wasn't long, another guy walked over to him, they shook hands, not really friends, but they knew each other."

"Did you recognize the guy?"

"No."

"How old was he, do you remember? Did he look like a friend of Alex, maybe a lifeguard or a, I don't know, a baseball player from the Cape May team?"

"No, he was older. He looked about 40-something. They talked for a while and Alex, I could tell, started to get that look."

"What look?"

"I didn't know it then, but I got used to it later. It's that look he gets when someone is trying to take advantage of him, ply him for information by pretending to be a friend."

"So, what do you think was happening?"

"It was probably a member of the Cape May Gym trying to get free advice."

"Did Alex tell you that?"

She shut down a little bit. "Yeah, maybe, I don't remember to be honest."

"Okay. How did you two meet?"

"Well, after a few minutes, like I said, Alex got that 'look' and his face got smaller, less animated and then he did his Alex thing, his face went completely blank and he wasn't looking at the man anymore. He looked around the room, completely bored, and then he saw me.

"So, I don't know what he said to the man, but he punched him lightly on the arm as he slid off the stool, nodded his head at something, and walked over to me and Lori Beth. He sat down as if he knew us and said, 'Ladies, don't get alarmed, but I had to get out of there. That motherfucker talking to me was trapping me in. He wouldn't shut up. Act like you know me.'"

"And what did you do?"

"With those eyes? I sure as hell acted like I knew him!" Abigail surprised herself at her own energy. "Mr. MacNeil, I don't know what to say, Alex and I were dating for a couple of months and then," she swore under her breath, "*this* happened. I feel like I could be killed just by knowing him!"

She tried, inadvertently to curl up in a ball and maybe caught herself looking childish. "I'm scared."

"You're doing the best thing by coming here," MacNeil encouraged her. "The more I find out about Alex, the more I can hone in on who killed him. He seemed to be very elusive despite his sex appeal."

159

He noticed that she didn't know what 'elusive' meant and he saw her eyes going through a rolodex of possible definitions and finally, wondering if she should ask him point blank.

"Did Alex have a lot of friends?"

"Friends?"

"Did he have a group of men or other couples he hung with? Did he take you to a party of someone he knew?" MacNeil ran out of examples. "Friends."

"Alex always had good vibes. He talked to everybody."

"But no one in particular, do you know?"

"Alex was cool. If he hung with one guy over another, I wouldn't know."

"How often did you see Alex?"

She shrugged, not so much that she didn't care about Alex, it was, it seemed, as if keeping records or noticing patterns wasn't her specialty. MacNeil wondered about her bank account.

"What does that mean?" he said referring to her shrug.

"It was a cool relationship, man, that's all. We hung out, he didn't want to be tied down, neither did I. No ropes. Sometimes a few days would go by, and I wouldn't see him. I'd drive by his pad, but his car wouldn't be there. Then, out of nowhere, he'd call, or he'd show up at Della's to see how I was doing. I don't know, god, we both liked the freedom."

"Did he ever tell you where he had gone?"

"I never asked. Hey, he was cool, he did his own thing. I did mine."

"Did Alex ever get angry with you, or violent?"

She looked surprised as if he had asked her if Alex had handled poisonous snakes.

"No! Never. Sometimes cold, no, that's the wrong word," she looked at the upper window, "what's that called, when he's in the room, but not in the room at the same time?"

"Aloof? That didn't bother you?"

The search in the rolodex.

"Have you ever been inside his apartment?"

She looked down for a minute and her face got red. "Yeah, a few times."

"Did you spend the night?"

"God, no. My landlords would have kicked me out if they saw me driving in at seven in the morning. I had to play it cool."

"So, you could drive home at two in the morning, and they wouldn't care?"

"Nah, I don't think so. They don't watch me, they give me my space, but overnight, if they woke up in the morning and didn't see my car, they would have freaked."

Hell, you and Alex could fuck at two in the afternoon, why make it more complicated.

"Miss Starbird, where did you grow up?"

"New Haven."

"Did you go to college?"

"Yeah, for a year, but," her breath got a little flushed, clearly embarrassed, "it was too hard for me, so I quit."

161

"And you came here?"

"Yes."

"Why?"

"Why?"

MacNeil pressed it. "Yeah, why here? What was it about Cape May that you wanted?"

Her face softened for a bit. "It's a beautiful place, Mr. MacNeil. The beach, the boys," she giggled, "I wanted to be on my own. The rent is cheap. Della's is okay, it's better in the summer, they tell me, when it's crowded. I'm thinking of working the arcade on the beach, or cleaning the hotels part time." She stopped to find a final statement. "I like it here."

MacNeil took down her phone number to check against Alex's phone records. "You still have my card?"

"No," she made a feeble attempt at opening her bag, "I lost it."

He reached into his jacket. "Here's another one. Please, Miss Starbird, if anything pops up in your memory, some event, some man Alex told you about who had any kind of beef against him, please call me. It could be a word, or an action, or something Alex said, anything to tip you off that Alex was in danger, please call me." He felt desperate using all these examples, but it was clear Abigail Starbird was overwhelmed, the office, the interview; she probably had been up since 4 in the morning working the breakfast/lunch shift. "Please call me."

"Is anyone going to kill me, too?"

"I don't think so. But, if you ever see someone following you or harassing you at the counter or standing outside your studio, you call me, doesn't matter what time it is." He rose and instinctively held out his hand. She didn't know what to do with this, so she flashed him a "peace" sign, slung her shoulder bag over her arm and walked out. She went in the wrong direction down the hallway.

"It's the other way!" MacNeil shouted and she must have heard him because she shadowed back across his doorway and headed out to the lobby.

Chapter 25

MacNeil took off his jacket and rolled up his sleeves. More reports to type up, more filing.

4:36. He had an interview with Ray Dieter, the Boy Scout Troop leader at 5:45 and he couldn't remember if Dieter was coming here or he was driving over to his house. He felt clammy, somehow distracted and he couldn't figure out why. He went to the men's room again, splashed more water on his face and neck, looked in the mirror. He hoped he wasn't coming down with something. Back at his desk, he took two aspirin and tried to clear his head. He made notes of his interview with Abigail Starbird.

Alex Kearney. The complexity of a human. Boy scout and porn actor. Both sides of the same coin? Warm, smiling, good-looking, then cold, aloof. He chided himself. *Just because someone's good looking doesn't mean he has to be on stage all the time. He owes nobody anything.*

He called Ray Dieter's home phone number and an older sounding boy answered the phone. He said his dad was getting home at 5 PM, but had a meeting with a cop.

Question solved. He closed the window, locked the office and said good-night to the front desk.

Dieter lived on New York Avenue, so MacNeil used the extra time to walk. He purposely forgot to put on his jacket, but his badge was in his pocket. He didn't try to straighten his tie; he wanted the most casual encounter possible. If Dieter had killed Alex, he didn't want to come in with any aggression, any predictable 'this is how private dicks dress in the movies' type of look.

Besides, I'm not a private dick, just a dick.

He laughed at his own stupid joke. New York Avenue wasn't too far, but far enough where he could think. He took the longer route, down Jefferson to the ocean and a left on Kearney.

Kearney, again. It was, despite the name and the circumstances, a beautiful street.

He processed and recalled the conversations, the interviews. The truth lay beneath the words, he had learned from his years in Buck's County. It's never about the words, it's about the demeaner, the look, the posture. Yes, a lie was discovered, a statement proved false, and that contributed to the evidence needed to arrest, but it wasn't the only thing.

"You can't bust someone on a hunch, on a gut response, MacNeil," his supervisor used to say.

"I know, but there's something bigger happening, it's in the aura, it's in the energy of the person," he answered when he was convinced who had killed the actor found in the canal but had no proof. But the certainty in his stomach said it all.

"Find the proof, MacNeil," his supervisor said, bored with the Hippie Dippy bullshit, walking away, stomach extended over his belt, coffee cup number twelve in his hand. "Everything else is just fucking nonsense."

560 New York Avenue was a small blue house, neatly grassed, bushes trimmed, and a small porch in the front with summer chairs already placed outside. Around back was a tree house and a patio made out of large flat stones placed in among the grass. Over time, the stones had sunk in, so that the surface was really quite classy, gray and tan flat stones that gave the area a little lift. Patio furniture was coming out slowly, a picnic table and two benches, and he saw only one Adirondack chair. Summer was a few weeks away.

Ray Dieter opened the front door and bounded down the porch stairs, walking rather like a Leader, hand extended, clearly wanting to be the one who set the tone, the questioning, the answering.

"Detective MacNeil?" he asked ambling over, large strides wearing twelve size shoes. He grasped the detective's hand and shook it hard. "Thank you for coming over." He turned behind him and two young boys were in the doorway, staring at MacNeil, waiting for a gun or a badge or the sight of handcuffs. It was like watching an episode of "Starsky and Hutch" in real time.

"That's Jeremy and Tom," he said, looking over his shoulder. "They know you're a cop, but then I told them you're a detective and they think that's even hipper."

MacNeil smiled and nodded toward the boys, not giving any on his cards away. Ray Dieter's grip was strong, the man looked like he had just changed his clothes. He was wearing a black golfing shirt and clearly, MacNeil saw, it was to show off his biceps, his pecs, his stomach. Not an ounce of fat. That type of 'father' that a son would look up to, unless the man had a temper that flared at the slightest provocation or he socked his kids or hit his wife, or both. It could go either way. Often it did.

"I'd prefer to talk to you about Alex out here away from your children, if you don't mind."

"Yeah, go ahead." He turned back. "Boys, back inside, and Jeremy, shut the door." He walked with MacNeil down to the end of the driveway.

"You were a client of Alex Kearney," MacNeil pretended to look through his notes, pen in hand. "When did you start training with him?"

Dieter smiled. "God, I think I was his first," he paused, "I'd say it was late September of last year."

"How often did you train with him?"

"At first, it was once a week, then it became about every ten days or so, I can't say exactly. I can look at my bank statements to find out."

"So, he must have been pretty good?"

"Alex," the man shook his head, "man, he was a good guy. Yeah, he knew his work, no bullshit. And he didn't take 'that's good enough' for an answer.

"On the first day I was with him, I have to admit, I half expected this over bloated military ego shit. I paid my bucks and thought, 'I'm too old for the drill sergeant attitude', but he wasn't like that at all. Shook my hand, looked me in the eye, asked me what I wanted to accomplish, wrote it down even. He took it seriously, and didn't try to sell me the Brooklyn Bridge. He was practical and he took my height and weight and gave strong pointers.

"After a few weeks, I saw the way he worked with me and some of the other men and I thought he'd be good with the Boy Scouts. So, I asked him if he wanted to be the overseer to two badge earnings: Exercise and Electricity. It wasn't a big commitment, he said 'yes' and to let him know what he had to do and that was that."

"This is Boy Scout Troop #245, correct?"

"Correct."

"What did Alex do? Did he go to every Scout meeting? Was he made a member and wore a uniform?"

"No, nothing like that. He came to the next meeting after he said 'yes' and I introduced him to the boys and said that if anyone wanted to earn his Exercise or Electricity Badge, talk to Alex."

"I never was a boy scout, Mr. Dieter, can you explain how they get a badge?"

"There are badges they can earn in pretty much anything. The Organization sends you the information. With Alex, if someone wanted to earn an Exercise Badge, they had to prove it by doing some many pushups and sit ups and weight lifting, those types of demonstrations, and you had to have someone qualified in that to sign his name to prove the kid did those things in front of you and did them correctly."

"A few pushups? Pick up a weight and do ten biceps lifts? *That* gets you a badge?"

"No, it's more complicated than that. Alex volunteered to help. There were only two boys in our troop that wanted to pursue that badge. He met with them, mostly at the meeting, sometimes they went to the Cape May Gym with me, I had to vouch for their supervision, and during my dime, he watched and coached them. The boy had to be a certain age and had to demonstrate physical training skills that matched his weight. Alex made sure that was all happening according to the guidelines. They also had to know about caloric intake and how much fruit and vegetables and grains and sugars to eat and what they did in the body, a general understanding of nutrition. Alex helped them understand all of that."

"Did they pass the exam and get their badge?"

Ray Dieter beamed, clearly enjoying the little achievements of his troop. "Yeah, they did! Alex gave them the test and some of it was in writing and some of it was at the gym. He gave it the green light." The man exhaled with a tad bit of embarrassment. "It wasn't a lot of skin off of Alex's nose, Detective. He did it for fun."

"And the Electricity Badge?"

"Alex told me that he learned a great deal in the Coast Guard about electric wiring and batteries and charges, etc, and the Boy Scouts have a badge that exemplified that. There was only one boy interested however, and again, Alex spent some time teaching the kid some of the basics, batteries, how to build and light a lamp, charges, dangers of electricity, I forget all the requirements on the list. The kid has to demonstrate his knowledge enough for Alex to give approval."

"Where did Alex meet with this boy?"

"Nowhere. It was during a few of the Scout meetings."

"What's 'Christ's Carpenters'?"

"After seeing how good he was with these kids, I told Alex about "Christ's Carpenters": it's a volunteer group I started made up of people from different denominations who have some skill to offer people who can't afford house repairs. Some of them had wiring problems, or faulty wiring, and since that was Alex's expertise, we felt he was qualified to help."

"Don't you have to be licensed by the state to do that?"

"I don't know, Detective, we use our skills to help people improve their homes, their lives. Decorating, painting, roofing sometimes, insulation, walls, hell even washing a car. If we ever got over our head, we backed off and called in the professionals. Many of us *were* the professionals, so, we didn't get any flak from the state. Alex was certified in Electricity from the Coast Guard."

"All for free?"

"Yep."

"Do you think Alex took money on the side?"

"He's not supposed to. Now whether he did or not, I don't know. I'd like to think he had more integrity."

"Did he ever show up in a bad mood?"

"Where, for the Boy Scouts?"

"Yeah, or for Christ's Carpenters or one of your trainings. Did you ever see him in a funk or a foul mood or being aloof?"

The man stopped his Boy Scout cheerleading jabbering for a minute. "Not that I noticed, Detective. Not with the Boy Scouts. The volunteering for Christ's Carpenters was a bigger group. We met at the Presbyterian Church basement, the jobs got handed out and everyone dispersed. I didn't always work on the same job as Alex, so if he was in a bad mood during the initial meeting, I didn't notice. My philosophy is, 'If you don't want to be here, then don't come. No one wants to hear your bullshit.'"

A car drove by and honked at Ray. He looked up, recognized the car, nodded his head, and turned back to MacNeil in a quick enough manner that told the driver, 'don't stop, too busy.'

"Do you know a man named Wendell Taylor?"

"Wendell?" Ray Dieter was surprised at the curve ball. "Yeah, a lot of people know Wendell, he works at Gaebel's."

"Is he part of Christ's Carpenters?"

"Yeah," Dieter looked away, "sometimes."

"What does that mean? You're the head of the organization, is that correct?"

"Yep." Mr. Dieter shuffled for a moment. "I don't know Wendell that well, it seemed that some of the volunteers didn't always like being around him. He knows his stuff, I'll give you that, but…."

"But, what?"

"He's a lone wolf. I think people were expecting more of a team effort. When I paired him up with other people, they'd come back later and say, 'don't pair me up with him again!' So, I didn't. The last thing I needed was for this great group to dissolve because of one man."

"Was Wendell belligerent? Bossy? Did they say?"

"Uncommunicative. He's used to doing everything on his own, in his own manner and timing. Trying to coordinate a task with another person, I think Wendell didn't know how to do that. Except with Alex."

"Alex?"

"Sometimes, I'd put him and Alex together for a wiring job and they hit it off fine. Maybe it's because they knew each other from the gym. I don't know, but one time I asked Alex after a job if he had any kinks with Wendell, and he said, 'Wendell?! That guy!? No, should there be?'"

"I dropped it after that. I either put Wendell with Alex or I let Wendell work alone."

"Did you ever get the idea that Alex and Wendell were, I don't know, scheming something, or did you ever see them coming back from a job with whiskey or beer on their breath? Anything out of the ordinary?"

"No. You have to remember these volunteers enter people's homes with the people right there in the house. It's not as if the place is empty and the volunteers can rob them blind. So, when Alex and Wendell were together, they had to have the owners there too, ask them where the fuse box was, or to shut off a system, and make sure everything got turned on properly when they left. If they had been doing anything shady, I would have eventually found out about it and they'd be gone."

"Well, one of them is."

The detective pretended to look through his notes again.

"Did Alex volunteer anywhere else that you know of?"

"Not that I know of. They're a bunch of people collecting a ton of artifacts for this proposed Cold Spring Village re-creation, did you hear about that? They want to create a village like it was in the 19th century and right now it's in the planning stages, collecting things, cleaning them, categorizing them and Alex may have gone over there to help out."

He changed tactics. "Did you and Alex ever hang out?"

"You mean outside of the gym?"

"Yeah, go to a bar, invite him to a poker game or go bowling…" he was getting tired of these stereotypes.

"No," Ray Dieter said and the lie was as obvious as a sand dune.

"Did he ever confide in you about women or drugs, or taxes or cars, anything other than weight lifting and strength building?"

"Around the boy scouts? Christ, no."

That's an interesting deflection.

"At the gym?"

"Oh, yeah, we shot the breeze, but I hired him to train me, Detective, not to be his counselor."

"Sometimes younger men talk to older men about life and the gym is a pretty safe place to bring something up. Did he?"

"Not that I remember, Detective. We met up, he trained me hard, made me focus. I wasn't there to talk about his sex life or his money woes."

"Did he have money woes?"

"I don't know, Detective."

MacNeil nodded his head. "Do you think Alex sold drugs?"

"He might have, Detective, he might have. I don't know."

"Did Alex have a gambling problem? He sometimes went to AC for a couple of days."

"Hell, Detective, I go to AC for a couple of days. I don't know if he had a gambling *problem*, but honestly, I didn't know him that well. He never talked about it with me, and if I had known that or known he was selling drugs to be a fact, he wouldn't have been in any Boy Scout meeting, I promise you."

175

"Mr. Dieter, between you and me, have you gone to any strip clubs in AC?"

Dieter seemed unfazed. "Yeah, a couple of times. There are a lot of them up there. I was with a friend of mine and we went in and had a drink. It was pretty seedy as I remember, the glass was dirty."

"Do you remember the name of the place?"

"No, I don't."

"Sometimes, Mr. Dieter, what I've seen in my business, is that people say certain things in an interview and they think they've told me everything, and then later they remember something that might be relevant to the case. Or they might not think it's relevant, but they tell me anyway. Anything could be important." MacNeil gave Dieter his card. "So, if something hits you later, a gesture, a word, a conversation, Alex showing up late, or stoned, or drunk, anything at all, please call me."

Ray Dieter took the card with the seriousness of a small part actor knowing his sons were watching him through a window. "I will, Detective."

MacNeil held out his hand and Dieter shook it. "Thank you for your time, Mr. Dieter."

Chris MacNeil used the ocean on his left as his guide to head back into town. He meandered the grid streets and once again, didn't care where his feet were taking him. It was 6:30 PM and it was getting cold and his thin shirt wasn't doing much. He passed the Chalfonte Hotel, walked across the lawn to the left side to the King Edward Bar. The white door was closed and when he opened it, a gust of smoke from the fireplace flew into his nostrils. The bar was warmer than before and MacNeil, without looking around, sat at the same bar stool.

"Maker's Mark, water back."

He closed his eyes for a minute.

Alex Kearney. Everyone in this town is so damn spotless. Alex never got into a fight, never had an argument, a loud nasty phone call, kicked out of a bar, showed up late for work. Everyone liked Alex. He's was so friendly! He helped old ladies with their fucking lamps! He helped young boys grow muscles and they must have worshipped his every move.

Yet. Yet! Someone hated Alex. It's one thing to think him an obnoxious big dick rooster, it's another to bash his brains in.

He heard the bartender place his drink next to his arm.

"On me," Matt Ryan said, sitting next to him, already reaching for his wallet pulling out a ten.

Chapter 26

"That's pretty ballsy of you," MacNeil snorted but accepted the offer. "How do you know you're not my #1 suspect in the Alex Kearney case?"

Matt Ryan leaned into the bar, a highball in his hand. "Because you and I know I'm not," he whispered. His shirt, MacNeil noticed, wasn't as loose as the other day, a more conservative look, but he probably adjusted that before he walked in here.

"You checked out okay. Trust me, we do our job."

"So I've heard."

MacNeil was getting tired of the game. Matt Ryan sensed that. "No, I'm serious," he said. "In the bookstore people are already making the comments, the conclusions. Most of them are women and their husbands or their boyfriends or brothers go to the Cape May Gym. They know about your team's interviewing and probing and they're impressed. They're running a bit scared, I have to say, some of them tell me they're looking over their shoulder, but they're impressed with your organization, your leadership. Murder is rare around here," he gestured to the sparse crowd, the quiet evening, the almost surreal surroundings of an upscale bar in New Jersey. "Most of the time these local cops get the shaft, stuck with traffic duty on the 4th of July or supervising Disco Teen Night at the Convention Hall in the summer. It's pretty boring.

"The men from the gym come in, too. They shoot the shit and want to know what I've heard." He laughed. "Detective, men gossip more than chickens, Christ! Some of them remember Alex and some of them, it's sick, *wished* that had known Alex so they could have something to say. Right now, they're lost in a news limbo. They all talk about one thing though:"

MacNeil shook his head. "His balls."

"You got that right. They feel that's worse somehow than getting your brains knocked in." He instantly, MacNeil saw, regretted saying that. "Sorry, that was uncalled for. I liked Alex. He didn't deserve to die at that age."

"Well, if you hear anything from these guys that seems odd, please let me know. God, Christ Almighty!" MacNeil rubbed the back of his neck and loosened his tie, "I'm running out of ideas."

"Why are you here?"

"I got a job here."

"No," he gestured to the bar. "Here."

"I want a place away from the police station. No one bothers me. It's small, relatively quiet, I can think."

Matt Ryan twisted his frame away, made a move to go. "Sure, Jesus, of course, I'm sorry I interrupted you. I saw you come in-"

"Sit." MacNeil smiled. "You're cool. I could use the company. All day everyone I talk to eyes me with suspicion and I give it right back. It can get intense. What are you doing here?"

"It's got a low, easy vibe. No music, no loud shouting of people getting drunk. I tend to feel like I'm Hemingway. Or Graham Greene. It's mostly a man's bar, especially this time of year. The summer's different. It's crowded and noisier. This, after the bookstore customers all day," he pointed to the five people sitting in the joint, "is heaven."

MacNeil gave him the once over. "How did you end up *buying* a bookstore? And why here? You meet someone?"

Matt Ryan laughed, "Ah, Detective, you got that look. What's your zodiac sign?"

"Scorpio."

"You got the eyes, those probing dark eyes that like to dig. Being a Scorpio is perfect for your job: mysteries, what's under the surface, keeping secrets, having a few of your own, good in the bedroom, unrelentless prodding, delving, not stopping-"

"All of that in the sack?"

Matt laughed at the misplaced modifiers, tipped his head in acknowledgement, "till you get to the truth."

"That's pretty accurate, I have to say. What are you, an astrology nut?"

"Nah, not really, I dabble in it. It makes for a good conversation at a party. I'm a Taurus. I like the feel of being someplace small, intimate, like this bar, like the store, like this town. I did the big city life, and when my Saturn Return hit, I knew-"

"Your Saturn what?" MacNeil knocked back the rest of the bourbon and felt for the water glass. The warmth was nice and he relaxed, finding it ridiculously easy to banter with this man.

"I talk too much. Skip it. I'll keep it cool. It's because I listen to other people all day."

"Maybe you need a few more friends and less customers?"

"Don't jinx me, I want more of both."

"C'mon, fill me in, what's a Saturn Return?"

Matt smiled, leaned in. "In astrology parlance, when a person reaches around twenty-eight, twenty-nine, the planet Saturn make a return to the spot where it was in the heavens when he was born."

"So."

"So, think metaphorically man, it's about stability, about what makes you a man, what gives you integrity, what lessons have you learned. You take stock. Haven't you ever done that?"

"All the time."

"There you go. So, when I hit 28, I knew I was done living in the City. Gave it all up, the money, the job, the sex – well, not really, - the boozing, the parties. I moved here, bought a bookstore. 'Why, for fuck's sake?' people will ask me and scratch their heads, but it's been my dream to do that. So, I did. That was fourteen months ago. No regrets. It's my Act II."

"Whatever floats your boat."

"How old are you, Detective?"

"Call me Chris. I can't be 'in charge' all the time."

"Answer the question, Detective."

"32."

"Ever married? Kids?"

"Nope." MacNeil looked around the room landing on two men in the corner looking like they were planning a bank heist. *Turn off the fucking suspicious mind!*

"So, did you go through the same experience when you were that age? Being able to call something you were hesitant about before? Able to look in the mirror and see a future with eyes of maturity, taking on more responsibility?"

"Half way through my job in Buck's County."

"What happened in Buck's County?"

MacNeil felt claustrophobic. The bar was still empty, but his back was hot and he felt the sweat coming down the sides of his chest. He finished the water and Matt Ryan took it as a sign. "Another," he gestured to the bartender.

"No," he waved to the bartender who had turned around reaching for the bottle. "I only do one."

"It's been a rough week-"

"I'm not much of a drinker, Mr. Ryan."

"Matt."

"Matt."

"How about we go get something to eat. I'm hungry, you are too."

"I can't. I make it a professional rule not to fraternize in town with a possible murder suspect."

"But I'm not a murder suspect."

"People don't know that. Thanks for asking, but I can't in this town."

"I'm not talking 'this town'. Stone Harbor. C'mon, I'll drive. They have a great Italian restaurant up there. We'll sit in the dark and you can wear a fake moustache and a beret."

MacNeil laughed and admitted his caution.

"I understand, Detective. You just started working in Cape May. Everybody's a gossip." He made a move to go. "If you want to count to ten and then meet me outside," he laughed, "corny, but…"

Chris MacNeil slid off his stool and headed with Matt Ryan to the door. "Hey, whaddya know about strip clubs?"

Chapter 27

Sunday. May 8.

Chris MacNeil collected his gun, and his badge, dressed in an easy pair of gray flared chinos and a blue and black long-sleeved plaid shirt, like he was going to a friend's BBQ instead of a series of porn theaters and strip clubs in Atlantic City. He wore a solid dark blue tie and put on a jacket he hoped didn't read 'two-bit detective'.

He checked in at the station and filled out the report saying where he was going. A routine procedure that he had to get used to, it was for his own protection. If he didn't come back that night, or the next morning, at least, if he was a corpse, they could track his somewhat whereabouts.

A yellow message note was on his desk. Ted Small had called and left his number. MacNeil sat behind his desk, and used the back of the yellow sheet to take notes. He didn't think this was anything important, most of the times people he interviewed would call him about any little thing that felt important to *their* eyes, but turned out to be something routine or vague. He asked for it, he knew, but there were times when some little, unfocused, predictable incident provided a clue to the bigger picture. And right now, the only pictures he had was Alex Kearney shooting his wad on dumpy dirty bed sheets and Alex Kearney lying there with his balls smashed like raisins.

Ted Small answered on the first ring, once again, like at his house, he had been waiting doing nothing else until the phone rang.

"Mr. Small, this is Detective MacNeil, I'm sorry I missed your call. What can I do for you?"

"Detective, thank you, I was hoping I could talk to you this morning."

The immediate urgency in his voice was a bit theatrical, something MacNeil was used to. It was like auditioning for an Agatha Christie play.

"I'm listening, Mr. Small."

"Do you remember when you said that if I remember anything, anything at all that seemed odd or different, to let you know?"

A bored director's voice. "Yes." He changed his attitude. "Of course, Mr. Small, so what popped into your brain?"

"It popped last night. I really, I really try not to snoop into Alex's affairs, Detective, I really didn't care who he brought back to the apartment, and I certainly didn't sit at the window at the side of the house like some old busy body, but well-"

"Hey, Mr. Small, no shame here. Everybody snoops, it's natural."

"But I wasn't *snooping*, Detective, I was in the dining room which I rarely used and I thought I'd give it a good cleaning, dust the table and chairs, vacuum the rug, wipe down the molding, when I saw a car pull up right outside. It's the only side of the house that faces Alex's driveway area."

"It's okay, Mr. Small. No need to apologize." *Christ, cut to the chase.*

"We both know what being twenty-four was like and I think Alex was no exception. He was popular, to say the least, I'm sure. But this was different. A car drove up and a woman got out. She looked around like she had the wrong address or maybe she was changing her mind because she got back into the car and shut the door, but didn't start the engine. She sat there for about five minutes."

"You were watching her for five minutes?"

Mr. Small stumbled, like he wasn't expecting a fallen tree limb in the middle of his driveway. "Well, no, I, I, don't think I was *watching* her the whole time, I was dusting the table like I said, but the car, the car, Detective, she *sat* in it with the strangest look on her face."

Well, bub, you were either watching her or not watching her.

"Go on, I'm listening." He didn't pry with questions although his brain was racing with ideas. He knew that to ask pointed questions pigeon-holed the witness: they stopped recounting and only narrowed in on what he asked which presented the ever-possible theory of missing something vital.

"I saw her take a long sigh, and pop open the car door and get out. She wore a skirt and nice shoes and she almost looked like she was going for a job interview. She checked herself in the glass window, then took a different stance, glanced up at Alex's windows to see if anyone was watching her and then, I know this seems odd, Detective, but she didn't stroll up the stairs, she marched."

"Marched. Can you be more specific? Was she yelling something?"

"No, she wasn't yelling or calling Alex's name that I could tell. She marched, like she had an agenda, a resolution. That's it, she was resolved and once she headed up those stairs, she wasn't going to turn back."

"Can you describe what she looked like, Mr. Small?"

"Well, here's the odd thing, she wasn't, it seemed, not from Alex's, uh, 'friends', if you know what I mean, not that I would know. She looked about forty, forty-one maybe, and her hair was neat and her clothes were neat. She wore a ring on her left hand and so I figured she was Alex's aunt or some other relative maybe passing through Cape May."

"Did she carry any luggage?"

"No. A small pocketbook or shoulder bag, or whatever they call it these days. A pocketbook, it was definitely a pocketbook, green, but small."

"I know this may be a stupid question to you, Mr. Small, but was Alex even home? Did you see his car in the driveway?"

"Oh, golly, of course, yes, *yes* he was home. His car was there."

"So, she goes up the stairs and then what?"

"Well, I presume she knocked. I can't see that side of the garage apartment, Detective from where I was, but I guess Alex let her in."

"Did you actually *see* Alex?"

"No, I didn't."

"Then, it could be possible he didn't let her in, somebody else let her in."

Mr. Small paused on the phone, thinking. "Well, yes, it's *possible* but I didn't see any other car there, but I guess Alex could have brought someone home the night before or earlier that day or…." He caught himself in his own trap. "You're right, Detective, anyone could have let that woman in."

"So, what compelled you to call me?" Chris MacNeil made a point not to sound impatient. He was thankful for the diligence.

"It felt unusual, that's all. Something in my gut. I don't expect someone of Alex's, um, appeal, to have a strange woman over."

"But maybe she wasn't strange to Alex, after all, as you said, she could have been a relative or Alex's father's girlfriend or God, the answers are endless."

"I agree. So, I pulled in my snoopy brain, but no, now, Detective, I wasn't snooping, but I went back to cleaning the dining room and forgot about it. I happened to be back in the dining room about an hour later; I thought I might as well wash those light curtains that were getting dirty. I started taking them down when I froze!"

I'd knew there'd be a dramatic moment. Everyone loves to tell a story.

"Yes, Mr. Small."

"The woman came back! She didn't march down the stairs, she scampered, light, almost like she was in a hurry to get out of there. She raced to her car and didn't look back. I didn't move because I didn't want her to see me or know that she was being seen."

"Did she get in the car and drive away?"

"Yep. Just got in and drove away."

"So what's so unusual about that?"

"It was her hair, Detective. It wasn't the same."

"What do you mean it wasn't the same? Was it cut? A different color?" He wondered if perhaps Alex did some kind of kinky hair salon styling in his spare time, like *that* was a realistic component to this seemingly unresolvable murder.

"No, it was the same, Detective, but it wasn't neat like when she arrived. It was mussed up. It *looked* like she had tried to recomb it, but wasn't very good at it, or she didn't have the time or she had to get out of there because something happened."

"Have you seen her since that day?"

"No."

"Was that the first time you ever saw her?"

"Yes."

"Did Alex ever mention her to you?"

"No."

"Can you describe her?"

"She was a little taller than her car, about 5'6 I'd say. Brown hair, I didn't see her eyes, not from this distance. Plaid skirt, brown shoes, jacket, I don't remember much else except for the green purse."

"Her weight or age?"

"Medium, I'm not good with weight. She wasn't skinny like a model, but she wasn't big-boned -that's what my mother used to say – only a little bit wide in the hips, a little bit."

"Don't try to pretty her up, Mr. Small, just be honest."

"I tend to do that. I like to think of people as I wish them to be."

"Her age?"

"Like I said, about forty, maybe late 30's, maybe a good forty-five. Hard to tell, Detective."

"What about the car? What did it look like?"

Mr. Small hid his embarrassment. "I'm not good with cars, Detective. Midsize, I guess, had four doors, it was brown."

"Jersey plates?"

"I couldn't see the front or the back, just the driver's side."

"Year? Make? Model? Old? New?" *Stop. You're being a bully.*

Silence.

"I don't know. Oldish, I guess, it wasn't shiny, it wasn't," he paused, "anything."

"Okay, that's fine, Mr. Small. Now, when she got in the car, did Alex come down after her?"

"No, Alex didn't come out at all. I mean he must have come out eventually, but nothing that I noticed. I internally chided myself for going this far and God, Detective, it does get depressing if the highlight of your day is checking out the neighbors."

MacNeil finished writing his notes. "If you ever see her again in town, Mr. Small, would you let me know?"

"Of course, Detective."

"Thank you for your information, it comes in handy." MacNeil had no fucking idea *how* it came in handy, but he wasn't going to admit it.

He felt Mr. Small beaming over the wire. "Glad I could be of help."

"Oh, one more thing, Mr. Small," his voice got darker. "I know you may want to brag about this with a friend, but please keep this to yourself until the case is solved. It could tip off the murderer and you may not even realize that. I wouldn't want you to be in jeopardy." *Christ, he enjoyed using that line.*

"Absolutely, Detective. Thank you for reminding me." After a few more 'thank yous' and 'you're welcome', they both hung up.

He left the info for Ricca and Kurtz, asked them to double check on Wendell Taylor and go to Gaebel's Garage to verify Taylor's employment, all of this was something that should have been done yesterday. He told Peter Ricca to question Wendell Taylor again, from a hometown point of view. He felt his own obvious 'I not from around here' style kept Wendell on his guard. He told Ricca that if Taylor balked, sit him down, look him in the eye and say he was just following orders.

He walked back to his apartment, the Hatchback had a full tank of gas and he started his trek. He suddenly had a certain feeling when he drove to the end of Washington, took the loop around Gaebel's Garage and crossed the bridge out of town. It was like leaving Brigadoon. There was an undeniable trajectory, an accelerated thrust that probably was a Law of Physics where once he was on the Parkway, it was as if the town itself would disappear and never come back.

Chapter 28

Atlantic City. The skyline rose ahead and it looked like a sorry excuse for a bad matte painting. The clouds had descended and Detective Chris MacNeil, using a map and the list Ricca had given him, parked on Pacific Avenue, a centrally located strip of road and started his investigation.

The town was dark, grungy, and many of the people were dressed up, skirts, jackets, ties, fashionable shoes, talking with forced smiles, coming from Mass or else wandering around, tourists for a day, walking the Boardwalk, hitting a greasy diner, looking bored.

Every XXX movie house was a waste of his time. The ticket guys at the window, when he showed his badge, shut down. Stopped talking. Every question was answered with an "I don't know."

"I'm not here to bust the place, I don't give a shit about you, your movie house, your customers, your tax evasions, your sleazy money laundering. I want to know if there's a movie studio here in town that leases porn movies to you."

"I don't know, I'm not the manager."

"I'm not the owner."

"The owner ain't here."

"The manager is out of town, in Las Vegas."

"So, you don't know of any movie studios in this town?"

"No."

"Not that I know of."

"Nope."

"Can't help you, pal."

"Take a hike!"

MacNeil saw red with that one and reached over the counter, grabbed a sweat stained shirt and pulled back a fist to smash the slob's face. He saw the terror in the man's eyes and relished in that power, but, Jesus, flattening his nose wouldn't solve anything.

But it would feel great.

"What did you say?"

"Jeez, sorry, sir. I don't know anything about a movie studio."

They were all lying. He should have known this would have been a brick wall. Anger made him hungry.

He jumped up the stairs to the Boardwalk and found an Irish Pub that served Reubens. He sat inside, out of the sudden cold from the Atlantic, at a booth near the back and wrote notes. He thought about the strip joints. The names Ricca gave him included Storkey's Bar and Grill, The Triangle Club, The Madrid Club, The Jockey Club, McCrory's Café, The Night Palace.

Ricca said a couple of these clubs were for gay men, he didn't know which was for what.

He checked their addresses, some were within walking distance, others were tucked in corner backstreets near the Convention Center. One was on Snake Alley which didn't even show up on the map.

Strip Clubs didn't open until after noon on a given day, so MacNeil watched the pub crowd, tuning into the vibe of their lives, and eventually he drifted back to his own. Thirty-two. The Saturn Return for him was five years ago and Matt Ryan kept questioning him at the restaurant about returning to that time to see what epiphanies he experienced. He knew how to shrug off the pressure, and Ryan got the hint. He liked Matt Ryan and found a common thread in their take on life. He wanted to solve this case quickly so that he could…what? Start getting to know the town folk? Start making friends only to shun them again when another crime happened and they're on the suspect list?

Ryan had chosen the city, chewed it up until it started to chew him up and then settled for the small town. MacNeil had grown up in a rural logging area near Biddeford, Maine and faced his first epiphany where, after seven years of baling summer hay between high school and college semesters, he'd have to leave or get sucked into his father's world for good.

B.S in Criminal Justice to eight months in the Police Academy, tests, detective license, landing his first job at twenty-five in Buck's County.

"Jesus, take a look at the big man now," the first thing his father said when he heard the news, "wow, the big fucking dick in a little fucking pond!" grinning, drunk, with a huge undertone of resentment.

MacNeil's concrete enlightenment at twenty-eight. His father was not going to get better; he wasn't going to become remorseful or apologetic, just remain bitter and mean and drunk. Why he didn't come to that realization before, as one analyst told him, "was because you didn't want to believe it."

Was this the existence of every young man in America? Not to Alex it wasn't. MacNeil reviewed his notes and acknowledged that he and his dad were very tight. I guess as tight as a man could be, without telling him about doing porn. He smiled at the irony, at the ridiculousness of fathers and sons.

I'm sorry, Alex, you died like this.

But, MacNeil thought, Alex wasn't the Boy Scout extraordinaire either. God, we all make choices at his age, at any age, but Alex's life was such a contradiction in terms. The Yin and Yang of his personality, the dark and the light.

Ray Dieter lied when he asked if he and Alex had ever hung out and talked about anything besides weight lifting. Maybe Alex told him about the porn. Up to now, MacNeil didn't spring that piece of news on anyone, but then again, if Dieter knew Alex was shooting porn he might have quietly or dramatically removed Alex from the Scouts. Unless he didn't give a shit.

When the waitress came over to give him his check, he pulled out Alex's photo. "Have you ever seen this guy come in here in the last six months?"

The waitress was older, had seen the hard knocks of life and was waiting for the lull after lunch so she could count her tips in the back room, have a smoke, and walk home to her grown daughter and their small two- bedroom apartment. Her reading glasses were attached to a thick string that hung around her neck, like a librarian, and she deftly pulled them up to her nose, peering into the photo then looking out over her lens at MacNeil.

"No, can't say that I have. He's cute, though. Does he work the Boardwalk?"

"Not that I know of."

"Let me get Dave, he works with me on Sundays, he might recognize him, he works mostly the night shift." She put down her glasses. "Dave!" No answer. "Just a second, hon, I'll be right back."

She was gone, used to busting her butt and moving between the tables with ease and she disappeared into the kitchen. In a second, another waiter came out trailing her. MacNeil showed the man the photo and asked the same question. Dave whistled, "Jesus, he's sexy, does he work the Boardwalk?"

MacNeil shrugged. "I'm looking for him, at the request of his family." He flashed his badge easily, not trying to impress or scare anyone. "He seems to be missing."

The two restaurant workers were unfazed. They had seen enough cops and busts and raids and shenanigans in their town to write a book.

Dave stared at the picture. It clearly showed Alex's face and body and his smile was as bright as the sky. "To answer your question, yeah, I have." He smiled a wicked smile. "I call him 'Bulge Boy'."

MacNeil stayed cool. Anyone will say anything to get attention. "Where have you seen him?"

"Here. In the pub."

"Did you talk to him?"

"I tried to. I waited on him twice. Both times I hit on him but he didn't take the bait, or he acted like he didn't know what I was doing. Hell, in AC, everyone has a secret."

"Did he tell you anything about himself?"

Dave slumped. "No, damn, I wish, but he didn't. I think he figured if he started talking back to me, it was a green light to make the moves on him."

"Do you think he works the Boardwalk? Is he a stripper?"

"I can't say. He might. The last time he was in here, that I saw him anyways, was in March. I waited on him, and he was no different than before, except he was wearing makeup."

"Really?!" The detective was surprised. "Does he dress in drag?"

"No, not that kind of make-up, more like a skin tone, a base. It's what an actor puts on his face, gives it a strong foundation before applying the rest. He wasn't covered in it; he had wiped it off, but forgot to do his left side and part of his neck.

"I didn't want to embarrass him, so I leaned in and whispered, 'hey, I know you're not interested in me, but I wanted to let you know that you left some base on the left side of your face' and I pointed on my own face to show him where it was."

"What happened?"

"Nothing. He thanked me, acted nonchalant, strutted into the bathroom to wash it off. He came back scrubbed and red faced. It was cute in a weird way."

"And that was it?"

"Yep. Pretty much. This part of town is crawling with hustlers and gay bars because when all the high-brow fuckers moved out, the gay guys took over this neck of the woods. Since he was in here, I figured he was trying to make a buck. 'Gay for Pay' they call it. Snake Alley is where a lot of them hang out. You could go over there and ask around. Do you know where that is?"

MacNeil didn't, so Dave drew a small map. The alley was off of New York Ave. Every time someone mentioned a street around here, MacNeil only saw a large Monopoly game board.

He left a generous tip and gave them both his card. They looked like the type who had a bunch of detective cards, stacked on their dresser, or maybe they pinned them next to the work schedule on the bulletin board in the back room.

MacNeil had his list of strip clubs and it was almost 2 PM. The Jockey Club was right around the corner, small, in a tight corner almost under the Boardwalk. A single light hung over the red door and as with all these places, there were no windows. He pushed opened the door and stood for a minute letting his eyes adjust to the darkness.

He felt the ocean breeze on his back and heard someone mutter, "God, shut the door, man!" He felt the eyes on him more than he could see them. One person made a wolf whistle and he couldn't help but slightly grin, but kept his cool. The place was the size of small garage. Long and narrow, the bar hugging the right, a few tables on the left, and a small round stage on the far end. Already, two go-go boys, skinny, hungry probably, completely bored, or stoned, were gyrating and nobody was paying them any attention.

MacNeil didn't wait for his eyes to adjust, so he walked toward the bar and immediately banged into a man sitting on a bar stool. "Sorry about that," MacNeil said, holding the man's arm, not just for reassurance but to keep himself from knocking into the next bar stool.

"Anytime, stud," the man said. MacNeil used the compliment and raced his eyes to adjust. The shirtless bartender had a thick moustache and looked at MacNeil wearing his jacket and tie and figured he was another suburban straight looking for a blow job.

The detective held out the photo to the bartender. "Have you ever seen this guy before?"

The bartender barely flinched and took the photo and held it under a lamp near the cash register. He returned it and said, "Yep."

"Where?"

"Who wants to know?"

"He's missing and I'm working for his family."

"You a cop?"

"No, a detective." MacNeil showed the man the badge, once again, not making it a big deal, not wanting to cause a scene. "I'm looking for this kid, where've you seen him?"

"Here."

It's like pulling teeth.

"Is he a customer, or does he work here?" MacNeil laid off the machine gun questions. He flashed a smile.

The bartender warmed up, stretching a bit to give MacNeil a full view. "Yeah, he works here, he did. I haven't seen him here in a while, but I'm not in charge of the strippers."

"He danced?" MacNeil nodded to the boys on the stage. "Like them?"

"That's what they do, bub. He doesn't have any family, you're making that up, you looking for some head? I gotta tell you, you're barking up the wrong tree. Brick dances and strips but that is it. He does it for the money, but he's not gay."

"When was the last time he worked here, do you remember?"

The bartender shook his head knowing when he met a man infatuated with a stripper, no matter what he said, the straight never gave up. "Jeez, I don't know, about a month ago, maybe three weeks? Brick is a sexy fucker and he knows it. He usually works on Friday or Saturday nights, when the real money pours in. He has a big dick and he knows what they want."

"Do you know if he ever hustled? Did he ever do porn?"

"Christ, man, they all hustle, this whole town is one big hustle."

"I mean, 'gay for pay', did he ever do that?"

The bartender clearly didn't want to burst this hopeless romantic's bubble even if he was a detective. "I don't think so, man, I think he's pretty clean."

MacNeil felt like he was in an *Alice in Wonderland* conversation. Getting information and then getting obfuscation, when he realized the bartender thought he was in love with Alex.

"Thanks for your time, mister." MacNeil left and opened the door smashing it on the hand of the older man walking in. "Excuse me, sorry about that."

The older man looked MacNeil up and down, didn't even hide it. "My fault, I'm sure."

MacNeil went to The Triangle Club, two blocks down, and the tall black doors, when closed, illuminated the large red triangle of its name, but from a distance the triangle took on the illusion of a vagina.

Chapter 29

MacNeil opened the right door, and the lights inside were not as dim as the gay bar. It had a pleasant looking foyer, surprising for this, but the ever-present scent of cheap house booze wafted everywhere. A woman at the door stood behind a shabby counter. "Two Dollars." She kept the cigarette in her mouth as she took the bills. She nodded toward the red velvet curtains with frayed ends at the bottom and a large black stain at the top.

MacNeil parted the curtains, and the place looked like a second-rate nightclub set in a cheap Film Noir. The uneven floor had, it seemed, thirty tables filling the place. The tables closest to the stage were rectangular, jutting out like starfish limbs with eight chairs around each. The middle and back parts of the room, the tables were square four tops. The place reeked of booze, beer, and cigarettes and most of the ashtrays, even at the empty tables, hadn't been emptied. The room was dark except for the lights coming off the stage and he had walked in just as the latest act was coming to a close.

The woman had stripped and was racing around picking up her "I Dream of Jeannie" outfit and the crowd, all twenty-three men, were clapping and whistling. The atmosphere was like a fraternity house, the men standing and grabbing their crotches yelling, "Suck this, baby!" and the overall misogyny had the stench of a decayed cow.

He sat toward the back, away from the other men, surprised that it was this crowded on a Sunday and he knew it would only get worse as the afternoon wore on. "Hey, cutie, what can I get ya?" the cocktail waitress was standing on his right, and from his chair and her standing there in her high heels, he could have seen up her skirt. Her blouse was barely buttoned and had a stain on it as well, this wet round look that accented her right breast and MacNeil figured it was part of the act she had created for herself.

She was used to overweight Shriners and married convention goers; she was playing the role for all it was worth so she could save enough money, MacNeil guessed, to get the hell out of this town forever. When he turned toward her, her eyes widened in surprise. "Whoa, babe, you're a man I could enjoy!" she flirted, moving her skirt closer to his right shoulder.

MacNeil smiled, knowing that if he wanted answers, he'd have to play the game. "Maker's Mark, water back," he said knowing that at two in the afternoon he was never going to drink it.

Her crotch briefly touched his shoulder, a bare suggestion of a hump in the guise of writing something down on her tray. "Well, we all like a good *cock*tail around here. Be right back, stud."

The next act seemed more complex. The three-piece band of clearly hungover musicians hit up a slow tempestuous tune, more riff than anything else, then it moved into a melody that he had never heard before. Out from the wings drifted a woman covered in feathers, long peacock feathers and flamingo and ostrich.

Christ, those better be fake.

She was a bigger girl, voluptuous, 'Rubenesque', as MacNeil's grandmother once said in describing a stage actress, and the woman displayed herself proudly, as if she were the greatest sensation of the century. And in this tiny, tawdry theater, she was. A voice from the light booth boomed into a microphone, "Contessa De Luxe!"

The crowd went wild. The whistles and the cat calls, the shouts, there was no filter on these men's mouths. Everything they felt or the alcohol they consumed allowed them to feel, and their years of pent-up sexual frustration blasted out of their guts in a torrent of words. The band played louder.

Contessa De Luxe strutted the stage, probably used to playing to crowds of 200 or more, but she didn't care. This Sunday afternoon crowd, was just as important. She crossed the stage from far right to far left, looked out, met the men's eye gaze, caressed her breasts, her butt, her legs and arms while the music played.

"Here you are, handsome." A voice in his ear. She was not going to bray above the noise. She bent low and MacNeil felt her lips lick his ear and a breast on his shoulder.

"Thank you," he said. "What's your name?"

She saw the dollar signs. "Ginny. What can I do for you?"

He pulled out a picture of Alex and held it at an angle so the stage lights could light it up. "Have you ever seen this guy? Does he work here?"

Ginny pulled back as if a scorpion had crawled on the table. "Who wants to know?"

"He's a friend of mine and I'm trying to find him. His girlfriend thinks he might be around here and she's too scared to come in herself."

Ginny looked at the picture. "Yeah, I've seen him in here. It looks like him, anyways. His name's Brick. I don't know much more than that. I remember one of the girls fucked him, sorry, maybe you shouldn't tell his girlfriend, but she said he was all talk."

"Meaning?"

"He knows how to charm the pants off a girl, but he doesn't have much practice in, I don't know, connecting, I guess. She said he was in and out and had his pants on before she had time to think."

"Yeah, you're right. I won't tell his girlfriend. Do you know if he works here? Strips, I mean?"

"God no, the queers don't come in here. Just those pigs," she nodded to the drunk crowd down front. "He's one of her back-up boys," she nodded at Contessa De Luxe, "he and this other guy pose up there with her while she uses them as boy props. They stand there in their speedos and, when he's on, us girls come out and watch. He knows how to fill it, let me tell you."

"Is he, uh, performing with her today?"

Ginny was already bored; the attention was off of her. "She could tell you more," the waitress grunted and walked away.

MacNeil watched Contessa's act. Clearly, she had different routines because there were no go-go boys around her. He felt out of his element. The burlesque/strip show vibe of getting gigs, and gaining an audience was a lot of work. Setting up the routines, getting paid, doing what you can to stand out, be different. The "you gotta get a gimmick" push and shove of this world, a world limited by age and beauty and appeal.

This audience's animal DNA was all that mattered to them. Getting off. Feeling young, virile, but they could easily applaud an act as well as tear it to pieces. Cruelty was the motivation here. Some of these men, MacNeil sensed, knew they couldn't get laid with these women, didn't stand a chance. It made them angrier and although they catcalled and yelled as much as anyone else, under the surface there was hatred for these women, these women who had all the power, who could laugh at a man's sexual prowess or lack of it and walk away, ready to get back on the stage and show it all over again.

The act ended. MacNeil left ten bucks on the table, ridiculous, and he didn't care about being reimbursed, he wouldn't include it in the budget. He moved down to the front of the house to a side curtain with an exit sign over it. He pulled it aside and heard women's voices off to his left up a small flight of stairs that clearly lead to the dressing rooms.

"Camila Sanchez!" the man on the microphone boomed again.

He headed toward the stairs when a man came out of nowhere. "Nobody back here, pal. Go back to your seat."

MacNeil already had his badge in his hand because if he had reached for it now, he'd been dead. "Police. I want to talk to Miss De Luxe, not you, not anyone else. Go tell her I'm coming up."

The tough guy looked like a fifth grader all of a sudden and ran up the stairs and passed out of sight down the hallway. MacNeil waited. A female voice. "What do I have to worry about, send him up!"

The man came to the top of the stairs and waved the detective up. MacNeil was ready for a jump or a knock on the head, he stayed clear of anyone and followed slowly, with confidence, a fake bravura he learned in Buck's County.

The man paused at the last door on the right. Just past that was a fire escape exit sign that would come in easily if MacNeil suddenly felt cornered. He waited until the man left, walked past him with the expectation of a fist or a karate chop and when there was nothing, he stood in the doorway of Contessa De Luxe's dressing room. The mirrors were cracked and dirty, the counter had three piles of make-up, three chairs, and three sets of accessories: hair extensions, false eyelashes, some small props. It was like a bizarre twisted version of "Goldilocks and the Three Bears". On his left, along the wall were a slew of hangers on a strong metal bar. Costumes, as with the make-up, were grouped in threes: gowns, dresses, Persian pants, even a nurse's uniform.

"It's not all mine," she said reading his thoughts. "I share it with two other girls, who, thankfully, are not on right now. Sit down."

She had on a large purple robe. She was at the mirror, but she flipped her brown cheap stool around to face him and he took another one and placed it so he could put her between himself and the doorway.

"What can I do for you, Officer?"

MacNeil showed her the badge. "I'm not a cop, I'm a detective. Chris MacNeil."

"But you still work for the cops, right? You're not a P.I."

"Yep, you're right." He pulled out the photo of Alex. "Do you know this guy?"

She took the photo. Sitting close to her, MacNeil saw that she was pushing forty, the stage makeup and the lights had lowered her age tremendously. She reached for some cheap reading glasses and looked at the photo. "Yes, I know him. That's Alex."

"I thought his name was Brick."

She handed back the photo. "God, that's his stupid fucking stage name. I told him it was dumb, but he made it up and wanted to use it.

"Brick Harden."

Contessa laughed. "This business is so ridiculous. Who would ever buy that? Jesus, I told him, yeah, okay, you can't use 'Alex', but Brick Harden? Originally, Alex called himself Brick Hardon, but eventually he got embarrassed by that one and changed it to Harden. That kid makes me laugh, I told him, "What the hell, in the long run, what difference does it make?"

"So, how do you know Alex?"

"He works in my act sometimes. When he's in town, he sleeps on my couch."

"On the couch? Miss De Luxe-" He wanted something linear. She read his face.

She began, "He was sniffing around about four months ago, came to the show, weaseled his way back here, must have flattered enough of the waitresses and asked me if I knew how to get into the business."

"Business."

"That means a million things around here, Detective. Working the Boardwalk? Hustling? Stripping? Porn? Selling drugs? It's a dicey area in AC, Detective, I don't need to tell you that."

"So what did you say?"

"I was pretty upfront about my life, that's all I could tell him. I strip. I enjoy it. I don't fuck. I don't do porn. He used his pretty smile and flashed his bulge in my face, suggesting a good lay in exchange for some contacts. I laughed. I told him that I don't give a shit about his stupid dick. I get my kicks from the ladies, Detective. Lisa, another stripper, and I have a good thing going, we're quiet when we're not working. Hell, detective, truth be told, most of these women who strip are lesbians. They get thrown out of their homes, families don't want them, they're young, confused, they come here, many are lost, hungry. Lisa and I give them a couch, some food, we're like the fucking underground railroad, but hell, no one else is going to give a shit about them. After a lot of crying and talking, and seeing their future, they start to make some choices. Most of them get jobs in a bank or something, get together and share an apartment or move away. Other gals do what I do. They pander to those morons out there and let them hoot and holler for all they fucking care."

MacNeil nodded.

"In this slimy town, Detective, we take care of our own. No one else is going to do it."

MacNeil was still. "Some of these women don't make it, do they."

"OD, suicide, or they get married to some fuck wad who beats them and eventually kills them."

He let that hang in the air.

"And then there are the innocent lambs."

MacNeil continued, "Alex gets in here to see you. You talk to him, show him the ropes a little bit. Alex becomes one of your back up boys in your act, but that ain't going to get him far. He's also a stripper at the Jockey Club once in a while but not for sex. Why is he doing this, Miss De Luxe, what's he looking for?"

Contessa De Luxe dropped all her pretense. "My name's Lydia," she admitted. "I took Alex under my wing. It's not my nature to do that with every hustler who comes down the pike, but he's a good kid overall. He likes the 'danger' of it, I guess. He gets off on the kicks. I can read a con faster than a racetrack list, and he isn't a con. He works hard on his body, knows he has sex appeal, and wants to explore his sexual adventures in porn."

"Lydia, porn's a con. This whole fucking set up," he nodded at the shabby costumes, the make-up, "is a con. Men don't do porn hoping to get an Oscar."

The stripper nodded, admitting the ruse. "Detective, all I can say is he's twenty-four, enjoys sex, vain as hell, but humble too, and when a porn producer took him aside after seeing him here a few months back, Alex felt he had made a mark."

"Do you remember the name of the producer?"

"No, I never met him, actually. When I first started, they wanted me to do movies, too. Jesus, those vultures came in almost every week wanting me to sign with them. I never did. But I guess this guy knew how to persuade Alex. They rapped in the hallway for a minute, then they left."

"And now, Alex comes up here to do a shoot and crashes at your pad?"

"Yeah, he drives up about once a month, I guess, but he's always very sweet, like a puppy in some ways. He drove Lisa to the doctor one time when she had a lung infection, got the antibiotics, paid for it, brought her back. He cleans up the apartment, and he wags his finger at our germ ridden kitchen. It must have been his Coast Guard training. He even cleans the bathroom after he uses it, Christ! One night I worked a very late shift, and at three in the morning, Alex was backstage and drove me home. 'No cabs for you,' he said, 'they'll find you dead under a pier.'"

"Do you think he ever has sex for money with men?"

"No, but I don't ask him too many questions, but he doesn't seem the type, Detective. He strips in the gay joints, gets off on the attention, rakes in some bucks, but he doesn't hustle. I would have known. He's not that bright in some ways.

"Mostly I warn him about drugs. Do your damn straight porn, I don't jive the attraction, but I get the male vanity, and treat your co-worker with respect, but once you start shoving needles in your arms with junk, meth, or doing lines, you're done. I told him that."

"And do you think he does?"

Lydia paused. "No, I would have noticed. He, underneath it all, is pretty small town. He told me he has a job at a gym and lives in Cape May of all places, and nobody knows about his 'double life' and he doesn't want that to cross over. If you ask me, he keeps his nose clean."

"Alex is dead, Lydia. Somebody killed him last week in that gym."

Contessa De Luxe stared at the news. Her face was still and she turned her head, her sad eyes sweeping around the dirty ceiling. She looked at her hands and perhaps gauging the age of her body, the passing of the years, or the sudden inability to rely on anything permanent, her mascara started to run.

She closed her eyes at the sting and found a Kleenex. She wiped her eyes and she looked at MacNeil as if there was something more to say.

"Oh, Alex," she whispered. She reached for his hand and he held it.

"I'm sorry you had to hear it this way, I didn't know you two were tight."

"Why," she couldn't pull out the words.

"I don't know why," he said. "I was hoping you could help me and from what we discussed, you already have."

She crossed her arms as if to hug herself. "MacNeil, he's too young," her voice broke. "He's too young." She stared at Chris's eyes. "Look at me. I'm not kidding anybody. I'm getting older, I only have a few years left to be schlepping these girls onstage." She heaved up her breasts. "I can deal. I knew the score when I first started. I like the whistles, the attention, but eventually, those whistles are gonna turn to boos. I know that. I have other plans. I've saved money. I've invested some, too. Lisa and I, we plan to move to Vermont, there's a new movement going on up there. Women, together, farming, plowing, sheep." She laughed, "What a fucking stereotype *that* is!

"But Alex, Jesus, what did he *do*?" She shook her head at his memory. "I'd like to think he would have gotten completely over his head in this business if I hadn't been around to push the brakes; I tried my best. If he had been killed up here, I could see a whole list of possible motives, but Cape May, that pissant town?"

A half-drunk Stage Manager roamed the hall, "Rosa Yolando, you're on *next*!! Jesus Christ, where the hell are you?"

He thanked her for her time and gave her his card and said the usual words of calling him if she knew any more information.

"You're a good woman, Miss De Luxe. Thank you, in your own way, for taking care of Alex."

"That's what we're here for. We take care of our own." she repeated. "Take care of your own, too, MacNeil," she said, already turning her chair around, reaching for the mascara brush.

Chapter 30

MacNeil used the afternoon to check the other clubs. The Madrid Club was the only other one who knew Alex as Brick. He stripped there sometimes, flashing his body, but he was lost in the memory of too many young men who did the same thing. The manager couldn't single him out any more than, "He has a nice smile, and a large cock; the gentlemen like that."

A dreary afternoon. The clouds formed and although it didn't rain, it might as well should have. The detective crossed the water to the Parkway and instantly felt a sense of relief. It was like taking a shower.

Everyone makes a living, you self-centered prick.

When he got to Exit Zero, he pulled the few turns to get onto Pittsburgh, bought a coffee at the small barely making it hot dog stand and drove to the beach. He parked the car and walked up the dunes. The wind was strong, but he didn't care. The silence, the serenity. He did his double-edged dance of living in this Zen sustaining calm community and swimming in the underbelly and the dirt of it at the same time.

"What did he *do*?" Lydia had asked.

The coffee's second wind did its trick. MacNeil walked the beach, back and forth, pacing practically like some earnest actor trying out for Sherlock Holmes. He ran through the list of suspects, all those men who were clients of Alex's. Did he say something to one of them? Did he accidentally say something where the man, putting two together, decided it was enough of a threat to kill the kid? And why at the gym? If you're that angry or spiteful, if you're really, really that set on killing someone, why not invite Alex out for a ride, or meet him somewhere, or go to his apartment.

Because Alex wouldn't have gone.

Alex wouldn't have asked a client to come by the gym late at night. Not someone with that business stand point. How easy that would have been! You hate the kid, so you *wait* for him to invite you to the gym after hours? What's the likelihood of that happening?

Maybe it was blackmail. But who was blackmailing whom? A man recognized Alex in some grainy porn flick and threatened to …what; do what; tell?

Christ, where are we, junior high?

He got back to the car, drove home, took a shower. A basic cleansing of the energetic grime he picked up all day. His father used to tease and borderline yell at him about that. "Are you really that much of a fag? You can't handle the grim parts of life so you wash them off like they were sand? Got news for you, Bucko, life's nothing but shit. It never goes away."

MacNeil changed his clothes, wore a windbreaker, and walked to the Police Station. Ricca's notes on Wendell Taylor sat on his desk. Sunday staff was a lone cop in the lobby and MacNeil read what the sergeant had written. Nothing he didn't already know. He threw the papers against the wall, surprised at his own level of frustration, seeing a pink slip by the end of the month, a hand shake and a 'maybe you should think about a different profession' coming off the bored look of the Chief.

The case was getting colder every day. The detective was missing something, missing some damn detail that didn't connect, that was there, he knew it, but he couldn't call it. He paced again, opening the door, going up and down the hall, back and forth, fourteen steps to the right, turned, twenty-two steps to the front lobby. Fourteen. Twenty-two. Fourteen. Twenty-two. The cop on duty got off his stool, stepped into the back area, all the office doors closed, making the hallway practically pitch dark. "Do you want something, sir?"

"Nothing, Officer. Thank you." He paced up and down, up and down. Thinking, thinking. What was it? What the hell was it?

MacNeil slammed his office shut, so hard that the door rattled like it was going to fall off its hinges. He locked it. He walked two paces when BAM! The click.

"Goddamn!" he swore out loud. He saw it all. He saw the whole outline, the scheme, the sly, fucking planning of it all.

What he needed was the proof and that would take a couple of hours and some help. He unlocked his office and called Ricca and Kurtz and told them to be in his office tomorrow at 8 AM. He walked back out to the hall, relocked the door, double checking in his mind to see if any other stone had to be turned. There was one.

"Good night, Officer," he said, and headed toward The Whaler Bookstore.

Chapter 31

There were three customers in the place.

"When do you close?" MacNeil asked the moment he opened the door.

Matt Ryan looked up and smiled, "I don't want *that* negative vibe! Read the sign."

Chris MacNeil turned back and peered through the window. "In five minutes."

Matt moved toward the door. "You're pretty smart for a dick," he whispered. Back to his normal voice. "Come in. What can I do for you?"

A customer purchased a few books and left, the other two, sensing the hour, or the shift in focus from them to the handsome man in the doorway, scurried out. "Who's that?" MacNeil heard one of them whisper.

Matt Ryan turned over the sign to read "CLOSED" and pulled the blind. "Great timing, Detective and thanks for driving out my business."

"Go to dinner with me. Right here. Gloria's, on Beach-"

"and Decatur. I know the joint, Detective. Really? There? No incognito or cloak and dagger? What happened?"

"I don't give a fuck anymore, that's what happened. I'm hungry. Besides, I have some questions for you."

"About the case?"

"Of course, about the case. When can you get out of here?" Matt had paused in mid stride. Chris laughed. "What are you looking at?"

"Is this one of your aggressive Scorpionic tricks, Detective? You seem mildly, dare I say it, happy. Gloria's? That's a switch. Aren't you worried about being seen with a suspect?"

"I think I'm about to crack this fucker wide open."

Matt opened the cash register. "Give me a few minutes to count the drawer, and I'll meet you outside on the Mall."

Gloria's had an upstairs seating area with glass windows overlooking Beach Ave to the ocean. At the door, MacNeil used his best detective voice, citing an authority he rarely utilized and the hostess, wondering if she were looking at a famous actor or a CIA agent, put them at the table in the corner.

The detective had straightened his tie and tucked in his shirt to make him appear official and Matt Ryan laughed at the juxtaposition: his own clothes made him look like he was heading for a Happy Hour.

A waitress rushed over, perhaps prompted by the manager to not keep them waiting, "Would you like to start with a cocktail?"

"Maker's Mark, water back," MacNeil said and Ryan asked her about wines.

"Burgundy, Chablis, or Rose," she recited, proud of her modern up to date lingo on the class of now existing wines.

"Jesus," Ryan whispered under his breath. He had a reputation in this town and didn't want to be condescending. "I'll have a Smirnoff and tonic," he switched.

The woman left, feeling five years older than her twenty-two.

"I forgot that if I want a classy wine, I have to go to Manhattan."

MacNeil got down to business. "This is what I want to ask you. When I first talked to you, you said you saw Alex and Gwen Parker in Sid's Bar. Do you remember that?"

"I might have, I don't remember."

"Yeah, you do. You have to." He leaned forward. "You're not on the witness stand, Matt, but I have to ask you to think about when you saw this."

In his focus, in his drive, MacNeil had pushed his right leg forward and his calf was pressed hard against Matt Ryan's. The store owner felt the pressure, the firm presence, the sense of heat through the pants. He didn't move.

Matt Ryan took a breath. "Let me think. It was a few months ago. I *thought* it was Gwen, but I wasn't sure. It could have been somebody else."

"What makes you unsure?"

"I was pretty far away. And I don't see Gwen enough, rarely actually, to have a full picture of her. I didn't want to embarrass Alex by hustling up there and introducing myself. It was an older woman, like Gwen, maybe older, she wore a skirt, I remember that, and I've never seen Gwen wear a skirt, not at the gym anyway."

"Okay, so whether it was Gwen or not Gwen, it was an older woman. You said it looked like they were flirting."

Matt thought hard. "I don't want to embellish this, Detective, I would call it 'flirting' but it wasn't high school. It was more subtle."

"So, for example, were they touching each other? Laughing too loudly, leaning in too closely?"

"No, but it was pretty suave, Chris. In a place like that where anyone could see them, they kept it cool, but every once in a while, she'd touch his arm, or laugh at something like she was a sorority girl all over again. It was a bit embarrassing to be honest, so I stopped looking at them. I left, actually."

"Do you think Alex was picking her up?"

"Pure speculation, Detective. Wouldn't hold up in a witness chair."

"Tell me."

"No. I got the sense, because the place is not a pick-up joint for guys like Alex, that this was pre-arranged."

"Who pre-arranged it?"

"I don't know, Chris."

The drinks arrived. MacNeil sat back in his chair, and his leg shifted with him.

"Are you ready to order?" The waitress saw the top of the badge in MacNeil's windbreaker jacket, and she put on another three years. It was clear the two men hadn't looked at the menu yet. "I'll come back later."

MacNeil lowered his voice. "The best place to commit a crime is in full view of everyone else. Nobody thinks anything's happening because there's nothing shady. All above board. Alex and an older woman sitting in Sid's. Could be his mother, his aunt, his fucking English teacher, but *you* are savvy enough to read between the lines.

"The other night I was in King Edward's and there were two women, also in their 40's. One says to the other, *"There's this guy you should meet, he's right what you're looking for. He keeps his mouth shut."*

"What are you getting at, Detective?"

"Listen. Kearney's landlord calls me because he remembers an older woman driving up the driveway to Alex's apartment *in the middle of the day* looking a little, shall we say, 'sheepish' but going inside his apartment. An hour later she comes back out, a lighter step in her gait, and according to the landlord, the one thing he noticed was that *her hair was messed up*. If you're going to do a little stud work, do it out in the open."

"Stud work?"

"Alex was banging the ladies. Not for free. Someone was setting it up for him. Someone who knows a lot of the older,

227

married women in Cape May, someone who sits on fucking committees, been around, knows their frustrations. Someone who knows Alex's sex appeal, maybe not personally, but certainly knows a business deal when it falls in the lap. I'll bet you the two of them split the arrangements 50/50."

"Who?"

"Gwen Parker. She procured for Alex. Probably set it up right before the Christmas holiday. Nothing like a little "Ho! Ho! Ho!" to make the holidays bright. She entices the women with a little 'advertising', dropping hints, making innuendoes, says to phone her if interested, and gives Alex a little tip and off he goes to do his stud service.

"These women paid in cash; Gwen's trail I could never find, but I bet you a billion bucks there are certain cash deposits in Alex's bank account that start to look awfully similar."

"Gwen Parker then kills Alex?" The bookstore owner seemed impressed.

"No, not necessarily. Alex is the "Goose that lays the Golden Egg" for her, or in this case, the "Gander with the Bulging Balls". Unless Alex wanted it to end and threatened to tell John Parker about this."

"Seems dumb. What good does it do him? He stops getting laid and is out of a job as well."

"Do you gentlemen know what you want?" The manager was there this time, nosy more than genuinely concerned about their dining experience. "We specialize in our meat."

Chapter 32

Monday morning. Chris MacNeil was at his desk, assignments ready when his two assistants walked in on time, Kurtz half asleep with a donut in a bag, Ricca spic and span.

"Sit down, gentlemen," MacNeil pointed to the two chairs. "I want you to do this together, this morning and have the answers by noon. I've set up two phones in the spare office, tons of paper, and yes, Kurtz, even you, are going to write what you find out, down.

"Call the local newspaper in Oswego, NY. There's probably only one. See if it covers the town of Scriba, NY as well. It probably does, but see if Scriba has its own rag. If there's a glitch, call the Main Library in Oswego, they'll have the newspaper on micro phish in their records."

"What are we looking for, sir," Kurtz asked, pulling out the donut and eating it.

"I want the names and family connections of any young person, male or female who died from August 1975 to August

1976. Anyone between the ages of eighteen and twenty-two. Christ, hopefully, it won't be that many unless there's some sort of suicide cult happening."

Ricca took notes. "Names of the families? Meaning, parents, grandparents, aunts..." he trailed off seeing a fruitless amount of unnecessary paper work.

MacNeil explained. "Get the name of the kid. Get their parents' names and phone numbers. That'll be enough. Most important, is how did the person die? Car accident, murder, suicide, falling through thin ice, whatever it is, find out."

"Divide the duty, take different newspapers, compare notes, leave nothing undone. *Nothing*. I'm counting on you two."

Kurtz swallowed his food, "What does this have to do-"

"Everything, I'll catch you up. I'm going to the gym; I'll be back in an hour."

*   *   *

The gym was open, Gwen Parker saw to that. She sat behind the registration desk, the noise of weights and racks a small roar beyond her right shoulder.

"Good Morning, Detective," she smiled, "are you here to sign up?"

His eyes bore into hers as he leaned over the counter. "I want to talk to you," he spat, "you self-righteous pimp!"

Her mouth hung open in fresh surprise, but she kept her cool. She slid off her stool, looked around calmly to see if a client wanted anything, and when the lanes were clear, she moved into the office. He followed and slammed the door behind him.

"You pimped for Alex! You studded him out to all your lady friends, your committee members, your god-damned Mrs. Robinson's like he was an expendable bull."

"Is the whole police station listening in, Detective? Do you have some hidden tape recorder under your shirt? I'm not answering your stupid accusations."

He took off his jacket, slam patted his whole chest to show her. "Nope. No wires, no machines, there's nothing on my back, nothing in my pants. It's you and me in here." She stared at him with a slight smile of amused irony as she looked at the bulge in his trousers.

"This isn't cat and mouse, Mrs. Parker, it's a crime to prostitute someone for money. I could arrest you for that."

"Then why don't you?"

"Because you and I know so many things: Alex is dead, your lady friends sure as hell ain't going to admit to anything, and you can say whatever you want in here and deny it afterward."

His breath was getting heavy because he was getting angrier. "To someone like you who hated being pawed, hated the catcalls and the double entendres of the men out there, hated the double standards you encounter every day in life, you take an innocent man like Alex and turn him into a sex machine."

"That's a pretty dramatic monologue, Detective. For God's sakes, Alex was hardly innocent; he knew exactly what he was doing."

"Why, Mrs. Parker, why do this? Did you sleep with him and wanted to share the good fucking news?"

"I never slept with him, Detective, but I smelled a business opportunity when I saw one. He's a cash cow, the ladies are horny, and to be frank, his sperm never dries up. Give him a little attention, a little, 'Oh, Alex, you're so sexy, Alex, you're so *big*!' and he'll do whatever's asked of him. The way to a man's heart is not through his stomach, MacNeil, but through his dick. He made *money*, Detective. He fucked for the money; he didn't give a damn about those women."

"So the misogyny lives on, and you, *you*, the one who said, 'Men are pigs!' keep it alive!"

"They are pigs, Detective. Alex, too. But what an easy way to make a quick buck to play into the sex drive of a 24-year-old. He ate it up. They had their fantasies: 'Be the delivery boy, Alex; be my son's college roommate, Alex; be the postman, Alex.' That boy loved the attention. People have secret desires, MacNeil, there's a dark side in all of us. Alex was their outlet."

"You used people for your own financial gain."

"No, not *people*, Detective. Alex. His bank account is just as filled as mine."

"Don't you feel one ounce of guilt for this easy prey manipulation? What did you say to him that made him do this?"

"I said 'you have a big dick; we can both make a lot of money.' There was no manipulation, Detective, just the lure of constant sexual attention which Alex loved." She stopped defending herself. "Detective, Alex knew what he was doing. He wasn't fifteen. He would have been doing this for the next five, ten years if he wanted."

MacNeil dropped the bomb and watched her eyes. "Did you know that Alex did porn when he went to Atlantic City?"

"No, I didn't." The eyes never wavered; she wasn't lying and she didn't look at all surprised.

"Don't you see how this complicates things? Jesus, I want a list of the women he serviced, Christ, at least to let them know they might have the clap."

"I don't have any list. Alex used protection; it was in the agreement we made. I got a request, got the money, set up a time and place, called Alex, and the rest was out of my hands. When he was finished, there'd be cash for him here at work."

"And John never knew?"

"Nope. And there's no reason to tell him now."

"Did Alex ever blackmail these women, or even one of them? It'd be an easy way to make a butt load of cash."

"He might have, Detective. But I think Alex had a little more self-respect than that. He could get the sex any time he wanted, what's the point of blackmailing? How would he prove it? Take pictures? Have a hidden tape recorder? Alex wasn't that calculating."

"But it's possible."

Gwen Parker sighed. "Sure, Detective it's *possible*, but honestly, if one of the women wanted to kill Alex because of this, how would she get in here to do it?"

"Maybe her husband found out and he did it?"

"And how did *he* get in?"

"Was Alex blackmailing you?" the detective asked.

Gwen Parker wasn't surprised by that conclusion. She even nodded her head in awe like a chess player does when she knows she's been out played. "No, he wasn't. I think you're putting a lot of intelligence on Alex than he never really had, and I don't mean that to insult him. Again, who would he tell? John? So what? All John would do is fire him and tell him to get out of town or some other tough guy talk that they all like to do."

"Did Alex ever screw men? Were they ever in your list of 'clients'?"

"No, Detective, he didn't and no, they weren't. That was something he didn't do. He knew he was attractive and he caught the eye of a few of them around here, but that was it because anything beyond that surely and clearly would be a doorway to scandal, to ugly blackmail. He wasn't always that bright, but he was bright enough to know that. He got off on the attention he got from men, and you, Detective, with your detached, aloof, all business demeanor, you too would have gotten hard seeing his body."

MacNeil never saw that one coming.

"I don't give a shit, MacNeil, but you're not that clever. Men don't know subtlety, and you can come around with your bluff and your sex appeal to charm the ladies, but when you look a bit too long at my husband's jaw or his arm, a woman knows."

"Are you threatening me, Mrs. Parker?"

"I'm not doing anything, Detective except holding up a mirror. And frankly, I don't care what I see, it's what you see, sir. If you want to arrest me for sex, arrest me, but arrest yourself as well. Arrest yourself for your own dishonesty, your own lack of integrity, but don't come around with a preacher's attitude to what Alex and I, together, did."

"Dishonesty? Lack of integrity? First of all, lady, I'm not on trial. I don't pay money to sleep with men. My personal life is my own but let me set you straight: for who I am, I can get fired *instantly* like I was a piece of garbage, I can get blacklisted in my line of work and never hired again and so can most gay people, regardless of their jobs, and there's not a damn legal thing we can do about it.

"We keep our noses clean and for now, hidden. It's not what I want, but it's the choice I make so I don't end up floating in the Delaware. That's the cold reality of my life, Mrs. Parker: we're beaten up, fired, blackmailed, killed without any recriminations. Those are four actions, I can assure you Alex Kearney, however he lived his life in this world, would never ever have to face for being who he was.

"Right now, I represent the law, and if I had the proof, I would arrest you immediately and drag you out for all the gym to see. But we both know that I can't. I've got nothing, Alex is dead, and you won't give me any names because it would ruin your goddamn precious reputation in this town. We all make choices, Mrs. Parker, we all keep our noses clean or hidden because we know the consequences. We wrestle with that complexity every single day, on many different levels, and regardless of the insane *infuriating* society we live in, my personal life has nothing to do with this case."

The gym owner acknowledged the ambiguity. She looked at MacNeil in what seemed to be a new light. She sighed. "Alex Kearney was a good man, Detective. He had a good heart, but he also could be a dick. I didn't kill him, but somebody in this town did. I hope you find out who it is."

Chapter 33

The investigation lasted four days. Yet, for the killer, the plotting, the planning, the scheming, the patience of it all had been ongoing for weeks and weeks and weeks. When I look back on it, Kip, there's a two-sided coin, a Gemini like approach to a murder. From your end, it's a race against time (how dramatic is that!) and from the killer's end, it's the slow, meticulous unfolding of a plan of action that is absolutely and completely justified. Ask any actor who's played Lady Macbeth or Iago or any of the other great villains. A villain in a play never ever thinks of himself as evil. He thinks that what he does has absolute validity.

The words, the actions of all of us, Kip, who's to say what makes an impact and what's ignored. All it takes, it feels, is for one word, or one insignificant action to set off a chain reaction of someone else planning your demise.

And one could argue that all it takes is one gentle word or one sweet act of kindness to set off a similar chain reaction that leads to healing, or connection, or peace.

What power.

A power that a 24-year-old had no idea he had. Is there an age limit to awareness? Was Alex supposed to know? Was he as much a part of his own death as his killer was? His Saturn Return hadn't happened yet, if you follow that line of thinking, his responsibility in creating all of this is lost on him.

I'm sure most of us would disagree. "Be accountable for your actions!" is the buzz message of the year. "What you do comes back to you!"

Transiting from that wide philosophical view to a dead body in a shower. Bam! Connected.

When you arrested the killer later that day, do you remember the shock at the sight of the cuffs, the surprised response?

Chapter 34

By 12:00 noon, Officers Kurtz and Ricca finished all their notes, compiled their information and handed it to MacNeil. He looked it over, asked a few questions, but the information was black and white. He told the two men to go to lunch, and MacNeil, munching on a sandwich he made at home, reviewed the list. Two men had died in Vietnam, but the rest were all local casualties.

Martin Van Tassel, 19, shot. Deer hunting accident. November '75.

MaryBeth Hudson, 22, cancer. December '75.

Charles Foster, 21. Snowmobile accident. Broken neck. February '76.

Cynthia Morgan, 20. Fell off a cliff. Internal Bleeding. July '76

Robert Jones, 22. Hit a telephone pole DWI. July '76.

MacNeil read the list and an instant empathic sadness descended on him. The names of the young. A cold list of lives and their facts and he felt the utter lack of control he had over anything. Life, for these five people, was over, God, at such a wasted and horrible price. The names floated off the page and he felt them swimming around him. One of these names, he was certain, had something to do with Alex's death. Intuition mixed with sadness. Completely out of reflex, and unembarrassed, he said a silent prayer for all of them.

He picked up the phone.

Jeez, this is going to be rough.

Every "Hello, ma'am or sir," was met with absolute mistrust. "This is Detective Chris MacNeil from the Cape May County Police Station," created a wall.

"So?"

"I wanted to talk to you about your son/daughter if I may."

"Fuck off."

Usually he could intercept them before they hung up, sometimes he couldn't. He had to call them back and use a more friendly, if that even existed, tone, implying nothing was illegal or wrong, simply enquiring about their lost one.

They didn't want to hear it. They didn't care one iota about a murder investigation in a different state. They were grieving tremendously and when he asked them to recall how their son or daughter died, no one responded.

"Read the paper, asshole!"

"Not talking to you." Click.

"Leave us alone! If you show up with your tv cameras, I'm calling the cops!"

"You sicko! Martin's been gone for over a year!"

"You call here again and I'm calling the cops."

"You bug me again and I'm calling the cops."

MacNeil gave up. He looked at the addresses. He called the Main Library in Oswego and found a very willing Research Librarian, Ms. Wendy Stevens. She sounded extremely eager to help as if her entire college education for the past four years was preparing her for this detective work.

He first listed off the names of the five people.

"Oh," she said with a sigh. "That was quite a spell. I remember the Van Tassel boy; he was in my brother's class."

"And nobody thought his getting shot was a murder?"

"No, sir, it was an accident. Some city hunter from Rochester trying to be a bigshot in front of his hunting friends mistook Martin for a deer. Shot him right in the chest. Luckily, the boy never knew what hit him."

"Was he prosecuted?"

"Involuntary Manslaughter, I think," she stopped, "I'm not good with legal terms, sir."

"How about the others? Do you remember them, too?"

"In a town the size of Oswego, sir, yes, most of us remember them. These deaths stood out. MaryBeth had been battling cancer for around two years. She didn't go down without a fight, I remember that. The memorial service was huge. Christmas made it all the more tragic.

"Charlie Foster, he lived out in Scriba. I didn't know him. A couple of times, he made the papers because people called the cops on him. Charlie'd be out there in the dark at two in the morning, creating that noise and zigzagging through the woods."

"And he wasn't murdered?"

"No, it was an accident. Funny, someone had put a log in the middle of the snowmobile trail the day before, but Charlie didn't use that trail that night. He was in the woods, but he hit a tree."

"What did he do for a living?"

"I don't know. I think he was a mechanic or something. He was one of those high school athletes you read about, that at twenty-one, should have been further along."

MacNeil marveled at the reporting-like recitation Ms. Stevens gave. There were no emotions in her explanations. In her work, where a research question could be potentially sensitive or embarrassing, she was used to being stone-faced.

"Cindy Morgan, let me see, she was out hiking with a couple of friends. They had driven out near Cazenovia, let me see, what was the name, hold please, sir, I'll ask."

Before he could say anything, he was put on hold and could have counted to twenty, she was that efficient.

"Gorge Trail." She was back. "She fell off a small ledge or tripped over something, but she hit her stomach on a large rock. By the time they got her to an ambulance and then into Syracuse Emergency, she was dead." Her voice broke.

"Sorry, Detective, that was just sad. Cindy's funeral was huge as well. She had been going to SUNY Oswego and was in touch with a lot of her high school friends. They sat in the front row, I remember, and sobbed hysterically, and their grief was contagious. Three of the girls were asked to sing, "The Water is Wide" and they stood up front and got half way through the song when they broke down in wails. The congregation picked up and finished the song and I tell you, Detective, there wasn't a dry eye in the place."

She moved on. "Bobby Jones. What a trip. He was what you call, 'bad news'. We were in the same class, and he's been drinking since he was fifteen. Always in trouble. Kicked out of his house the moment he turned eighteen. Had a few friends, but most of them now are in prison."

"So, you weren't surprised at his death?"

There was a pause as if she was judging her own lack of empathy. "No, sir, I wasn't. I didn't go to his funeral. I don't know if anybody did."

"Have you ever heard of a man named Alex Kearney? He worked at a men's gym in Oswego for a man named Jim Crane."

A silence that made MacNeil tilt his head.

"So *that's* his last name."

"Ms. Stevens."

"Hold on for one moment, Detective, I want to go into the office and shut the door."

Gone. He counted to twenty but made it only to ten.

"Detective, I can't stay in here too long. I never met Alex, but I heard of him. He dated Cindy Morgan for a few

243

months. My sister is friends with Cindy's best friend and the only reason why I give a shit at all about these local girls is that *I'm* a local girl. They can get mixed up with some pretty scuzzy boyfriends. In a town like this, I tell the girls to look out for each other, take care of your own. Like I said, I never met Alex, but I heard he had a lot of charm. Cindy also made a point to not let any of her friends meet him or tell them his last name."

"Why?"

"I can make a guess, Detective. Some of these girls like the 'bad boy', the grease monkey, the body builder knowing damn well they're never going to marry them. It's a secret thrill. They go out, but not often, not in a public way like a movie or restaurant. Maybe they drive to some place where nobody knows them. For people like Cindy, it's a fantasy, the hot one-hour tryst, sex in the back seat along the lake, feeling like you have control over your life, like you're finally an adult." He heard the librarian scoff. "But what usually happens is the girl gets pregnant, and in this Catholic town, pregnant means wedding which means hell for the next fifty years."

"So, what has that got to do with Alex?"

"He knocked her up, sir. I'm convinced of it." The librarian's register dropped to her Oswego, flat-voweled upstate roots. "That kid didn't bleed to death from any damn rock, sir. Between you and me, I'd say she got a botched-up abortion from some two-bit hack, didn't tell anyone, went on her stupid, ignorant way, not knowing much about anything except that she had a pain she tried to ignore, and eventually, bled to death."

"There was no autopsy?"

"I wouldn't know, sir, but in this town, if something like that were to come to light, it'd be hell for the family. A few bucks to the right people and it all disappeared and reappeared as an unfortunate hiking accident."

"Was Alex with her when she fell?"

"God, no! She was with two close-knit girlfriends. I think they too had never met Alex, only *heard* about him, to the point where I'm sure they were beginning to believe Cindy made him up. Never met him, never saw him, never thought about Cindy getting preggers let alone getting an abortion." She utilized her New York City Columbia experience. "They're pretty naïve around here, sir."

"Do you remember their names?"

When she recounted their names, MacNeil thanked her, took his cuffs and walked into town.

"We can do this the easy way or the hard way," he said to Abigail Starbird.

Chapter 35

*T*he kicking. The screaming! The sheer panic of a 20-year-old. It made the local news, remember Kip? Your face, those penetrative eyes, focused, directed, the shot of you leaving the police station after locking up Abigail Starbird.

You used to beat yourself up for jumping to such ridiculous conclusions. She lived in New Haven and you assumed she meant Connecticut. It wasn't. It was New York. Ten miles from Scriba.

After her best friend died, so young, bleeding to death, she started to see the reality. The crap shoot abortion. A man named Alex. It could have been a fake name Cindy had invented, but she had to start somewhere. She contacted a few garages and cab companies, batting zero until the day she called a men's gym in Oswego asking for Alex sounding like some lost lamb. She took a chance. "The good-looking guy with the dark hair." Jim Crane, unfazed, told her, as he did a dozen other voices, that Alex left for Cape May, New Jersey to work at the gym there.

Abigail was ecstatic at her trenchancy. He had left for Cape May twenty-five days after Cindy Morgan died. Alex probably never knew *about the abortion, or if he did, he threw some money at her and in his head, moved on. He never put two and two together. Alex only knew one thing: Alex.*

She followed him. Took her time getting settled, keeping tabs on him. It was easy to call the only gym in town and ask if Alex worked there, but she was sharper than that. She'd ask, "When does Alex work today?" or "Is Alex working right now?" Anything to make either Gwen or John Parker give her concrete information. When they did, she'd easily drive over and laze about in her car like a predictable Cape May beach girl, no one suspecting anything being out of place. Even though she didn't know what Alex looked like, if Gwen said he was expected at noon, the odds were in her favor. It wouldn't take much detective work to witness a muscled young man entering the gym around that time. Alex would also stand out because he probably wouldn't have a gym bag or he'd already be dressed for training. A few more consistent sightings of the same man coming and going was enough evidence for her.

Stalking him is the word we use now, Kip. She made it a point to hang out at the C-View because she saw that's where he went most frequently. The chance encounter. The innocent conversation. All planned.

The slow dating, the casual sex, the live and let live of the '70's. She played the part so damn well, didn't she, Kip. Get in with Alex, but not too in. Nothing that would make people notice, but she didn't have to worry about that. Alex was friendly with a lot of women. It probably only fueled her justification.

How many more fucked up abortions are you going to be responsible for, Alex, how many?

The fun sex fantasy that she presented. "Let's do it in the gym, Alex! Late at night, in the shower! Wouldn't that be a trip?"

And Gwen Parker was right. The best way to a man's heart is through his dick. And Alex said, "Yes." He left the gym door open at the agreed time. Abigail snuck in. Alex was already in the shower. She picked up a weight. She was stronger than she looked. Years of picking up trays full of food did that.

As you presented to the D.A., she stripped herself, didn't say anything, pulled back the curtain, and knowing she couldn't hit him in the head directly, aimed for the testicles. Slam! We know that sensation and now double it! He bent over, looking at her in surprise when the easy part presented itself. She slugged him in the skull, then again, and again, until he dropped to the floor. She continued the work avenging her friend Cindy Morgan until he died. Then she pulled his legs apart and pulverized his balls. No polite way to say it.

The blood splattered on her, you guessed, but it was easy to stand in the shower, around the body, wash everything off. She found a clean towel and dried herself. She reached into Alex's pants for the keys, took off the gym key, wiped off any fingerprints, got dressed, and waited.

You estimated she must have waited an hour, pure speculation, but she sat in that locker room not touching anything holding a wet towel and that key. She waited. She wanted to make sure Alex was truly dead, looked for signs of revival, or a moan, or any movement whatsoever. She knew no one was coming in.

After the hour, she turned out the light, and left. Here was her only possibility of being seen, but she had worn, perhaps, darker clothes, a hat, opened the door and looked around. She locked the gym, walked to her car parked a few blocks away and drove home. When she crossed the canal, she tossed the key off the bridge, the towel is long gone in some trash can.

Brilliant deduction, Detective. Absolutely right on.

None of it stuck.

That's the irony of it. She was released in a week for lack of concrete evidence.

"Guessed. Estimated. Supposed. Projected." The D.A. shook his head, agreeing with you as you presented your explanation of the crime, but it all boiled down to evidence.

Abigail Starbird had a good sense of law. She said nothing. Not a blessed word. Her lawyer handled it. She moved to California in early June.

You were expecting to be fired, but it didn't happen. They knew this case couldn't hold up without the vital evidence.

A few pats on the back, the shake of the head from the Chief. The 'better luck next time' from the D.A.; styles of behavior most detectives experience again and again.

"You did the best you could do, Detective." If you had a dollar...

The intense scrutiny of life that you used to question: was it worth it? Do we stand in judgment of the Alexes and the Abigails?

Alex used women; Alex helped people fix their homes. He had a ready pat for any man at the gym, he did porn on the side. He protected strippers, mentored boy scouts, and banged older women for money. He took no responsibility for the life of Cindy Morgan because she was never on Alex's radar screen. Gwen Parker was right: the absolute dark and light within all of us.

Alex is buried in Scriba. Cindy Morgan is buried in Oswego. Two graves that should never had been dug so soon, so early.

You and I took some days off after that case, remember? Your boss suggested that. I hired another man to run the bookstore, and we went to the Poconos for three days to 'go fishing'. Lake side cabin. Cold swims; it was still May and we didn't care. Fireplace. Funky kitchen and an even funkier bed. Years later, we bought the place.

After all that time, Kip, the quality of our lives, the way we live, who's to be the judge of that?

My eclectic catholic loft at Cape May Point where I live now is my best comfort. Your memories are here, and often, my friends will visit and we'll walk over the sand dune and sit on the beach and watch the sunset. The serenity never ceases to move me. Winter nights I read, and write, and I light a candle and place it in the window so you're able to find me in the dark.

Your ashes are spread on the beach that no longer exists and life here, though quiet yet lovely, Kip, is furnished with the beauty of this place: the September serenity on Poverty, the snow falling on Hughes, and the silent, sweet whisper of your voice forever in my ear.

Made in the USA
Middletown, DE
12 November 2022

14791381R00146